The
FUGITIVES
of
GETHSEMANE

Also by D.S. Lliteras

Death Takes a Byline

Descent

Syllables of Rain

Viet Man

Flames and Smoke Visible

The
FUGITIVES
of
GETHSEMANE

The Three Days Following
the Crucifixion of Jesus

a novel

D.S. LLITERAS

RAINBOW RIDGE
BOOKS

Cover and interior design by Frame25 Productions
Cover photo © Romolo Tavani c/o Shutterstock.com

Published by:
Rainbow Ridge Books
www.rainbowridgebooks.com

Distributed by:
Square One Publishers, Inc.
www.squareonepublishers.com
877-900-BOOK

Library of Congress Control Number: 2022948530

ISBN 978-1-937907-74-7

Printed in the United States of America

Not ready. Never ready.
Nobody can ever be ready
for the death of love—
I swear, I wanted to be
at the foot of his cross.
I swear, I loved him.

—from *The Thieves of Golgotha* by D.S. Lliteras

"I will have mercy on whom I wish,
I will take pity on whom I wish."

—Romans 9:15

PART I

James the Younger

1

PART II

Matthew the Publican

61

PART III

Simon the Patriot

89

PART IV

Thomas the Doubter

117

PART V

Discovery at Golgotha

137

PART VI

The Women and Safety

169

PART VII

Nightmares and Dreams

179

PART VIII

The Women and Jesus

215

PART IX

The Escape

239

PART X

Toward a New Beginning

271

PART XI

Belief, As It Is—

279

It does not depend on what man wants
or does, but only on God's mercy.
—Romans 9:16

PART I

~

JAMES THE YOUNGER

Chapter 1

Jesus announced, "*I tell you the truth, one of you is going to betray me.*"

The twelve men, who sat at the supper table with him, stirred uneasily.

Andrew leaned against the table and stared at a bowl of figs. His dark brown hair was loose, and as thick as his trimmed beard and mustache. His piercing eyes revealed a fierce temperament.

Andrew scrutinized several brethren and discovered that they were also appalled by this declaration. He turned toward Jesus. "Surely you don't mean me."

"Nor me—"

"Or me."

"I'm innocent."

These whispered protests, which continued to spread across the disrupted table, prompted Matthew to shout, "This is outrageous!" He waved at his brethren in an attempt to further intensify their brew of resentment, and unify their pleas of innocence.

John stood up and raised his right hand as if he were preparing to declare an oath. His shoulder-length hair was as thick and as black as his beard. He wore a collarless tunic of brown wool that was tied at the waist with a leather strap.

John measured the earnestness of his fellow disciples, to be certain that he was in conformance with them in rebellion, before he proclaimed, "I *am* innocent."

As the din of indignation persisted among all those at the table, Peter leaned toward James the younger and whispered, "Ask our Lord who among us will betray him."

"*Me*? No. Not me."

"Go on. You're sitting next to him."

James the younger wiped his tight mouth with the back of his left hand in dismay. His dark brown beard was short and his mustache was carefully trimmed. The white linen that was wrapped around his head covered a portion of his medium length hair. He was a short and small-boned man with dark brown eyes, small ears, and a narrow nose. He wore a full-length sleeveless cloak with black and brown stripes over his thin and shapeless beige tunic. James had his upper mantle draped over his shoulders rather than over his head.

Within the increased clamor of the surrounding men, James leaned toward Jesus and asked, "Lord, who will betray you?"

Jesus beckoned him to come closer, then whispered into his ear.

James glanced furtively at Judas as he listened, then shrank away from Jesus. "But Lord—"

Peter grabbed James's forearm and pulled him away from Jesus. "What did he say?"

"*Nothing.* Nothing important."

He released James's forearm, then curled the fingers of his right hand into a threatening fist. "Damn your eyes. I'll be the judge of that."

A wild length of hair hung beneath the lower rim of Peter's linen head-wrap. His thick unkempt beard matched his stormy temperament.

When the pandemonium in the room crested, Jesus raised his right hand to establish order and silence at the table. Then he tore off a small piece of bread from an untouched loaf that was near a dish of sauce. "*It will be one of you twelve, one who dips his bread in the dish with me. The Son of Man will die as the scriptures say he will, but how terrible for that man who will betray the Son of Man. It would have been better for that man if he had never been born!*"

Twelve dozen eyes widened with distress, vexation, indignation, and self righteousness in response; these eyes narrowed suddenly with close attention when Judas involuntarily stood up and approached Jesus.

Judas's facial features were strong; his beard and mustache were short and well-groomed. His light woolen tunic was full length, slitted on both sides, and tied at the waist with a leather belt. His long wavy black hair was crowned with a tightly woven skullcap.

Judas raised his right forefinger to his lips as if he were preventing himself from having to speak, as if he were searching for a reason not to stand before his Lord. "Surely you don't mean me, Rabbi."

Jesus answered, "*So you say.*"

5

Judas accepted the bread that Jesus offered to him.

"*Hurry and do what you must,*" said Jesus.

Nobody suspected Judas to be the traitor because their Lord trusted him to be in charge of the common purse, and because he was often instructed to pay for their food at odd hours.

Judas ate the morsel of bread after dipping it into the nearby dish of sauce, accepted the cup of wine from his Lord, then leveled a solemn gaze at Jesus as he drank the wine slowly to its finish.

James was bewildered by what he was witnessing; he was never able to peer into his Lord's eyes for that long— and with such steadiness.

Judas gave the cup back to Jesus, turned away from him, and left the room.

James smiled at Peter like a demented child.

Jesus summoned everyone's attention as he set the cup on the table, then broke off a large portion of bread from the same loaf and gave a prayer of thanks to God. And as he gave a morsel of this bread to each man, he said, "*Take and eat it, this is my body.*"

James received his morsel and, like the others after him, he ate the bread while he was preoccupied by his confusion over what he was eating rather than accepting the mystery of this body given to him by his Lord.

Like the others, James was present, but not present— he was also burdened by the mystery of what Jesus had told him.

Jesus poured more wine into the cup, picked it up, and raised it above his head with both hands to give thanks to God, and said, "*Drink it, all of you, for this is my blood that seals God's covenant, which will be shed on behalf of many for the forgiveness of sins.*"

James was given the cup and, like the others after him, sipped the wine while preoccupied by his confusion over what he was drinking rather than accepting the mystery of this blood given to him by his Lord.

Again, like the others, James was present, but not present.

As Jesus continued sharing his cup with each man, James glanced at Peter, who remained puzzled by what he drank and, therefore, Peter was not present.

Then James looked at Bartholomew, who was too skeptical to have tasted what he drank and, therefore, he was not present. He scrutinized James the elder, who was too jealous of John to have listened to our Lord and, therefore, he was not present. Then there was Philip who, and Andrew who, and Thaddaeus who—all, were equally present, but not present during this sacred supper of bread and wine, of body and blood.

After everyone had taken a drink from the cup, and had been allowed to consider this sealed covenant from God, which lead to the forgiveness of sins, Jesus said to them, "*This very night all of you will run away and leave me.*"

This announcement startled everyone.

The strained silence that followed seemed deeper than the perplexed silence during their consumption of the body and the blood.

Peter was more distraught than the others. And when he caught James averting his eyes from him, Peter launched a caustic interrogation. "Why are you spying on me?"

James shrank away from him.

"What are you seeing?"

James bit his lower lip.

"Damn you. What do you know?"

"I know nothing," James replied.

"Liar." Then Peter turned away from him and shouted, "I'll *not* abandon our Lord!"

Peter found enough courage to stand up and face Jesus and pound the table with the heels of his fists. "I will never leave you even if all the rest do!"

"*I tell you this Peter,*" Jesus answered, "*the cock will not crow today until you have said three times that you do not know me.*"

"I will never say I do not know you!" Peter cried, "Even if I have to die with you!" He began pounding the table again and encouraged the others to participate: first Simon, then Matthew, then Thomas, then—James the younger, who was glad to join the steady beat and the growing chorus of resentment concerning their lack of loyalty toward their Lord.

James was also grateful that Peter had lost interest in the secret that Jesus had shared with him and, therefore, he pounded the table with dual enthusiasm.

Chapter 2

James the younger was relieved that he was no longer trapped in a roomful of confused and resentful men. He was glad to be outside and breathing fresh air, which cleared his mind and calmed his spirit. This sense of relief accompanied him as he followed Jesus and the others out of Jerusalem and into the countryside toward their destination.

As Jesus led him and his brethren disciples across the Kidron Valley, James glanced back at that intimidating big city called Jerusalem.

The formidable stone wall that surrounded the city was a high and massive structure with numerous bastions extending outward, and with square towers built along the wall at critical defense areas. And because the gates were weak and difficult to defend, towers were also built on both sides of the them. A parapet and a walkway ran along the top of the wall; the indented parapet provide protection and the walkway provided strategic mobility for the Roman Auxiliary Legionnaires and the Temple Guards— the power of Pilot and the force of Herod.

James inhaled deeply. And as he savored the clear air, he continued studying his surroundings.

The predominantly barren Kidron Valley managed to support modest populations of trees and shrubs upon small sections of its terrain; small portions of this sparse and rocky region also managed to support an uneven cover of scrub grasses and wild weeds.

The road, which led toward the only gate leading into the city that was presently visible to him, was busy with pilgrims who were traveling on carts and asses and camels—all, were hoping to reach Jerusalem before that gate was closed. These weary pilgrims wanted to take advantage of the city's relative safety from a surrounding countryside that was often full of dangerous professional highwaymen.

James directed his attention toward their destination.

The Mount of Olives was a two-and-a-half, mile-long, mountain ridge that dominated the geography on the eastern side of Jerusalem. Portions of the Mount of Olives were thinly wooded with clusters of myrtles and groups of palm trees that were scattered randomly on the mount. Numerous shrubs and thistles and vines also covered portions of the rocky terrain that were unoccupied by olive groves, olive presses, and well kept gardens like Gethsemane that were enclosed by low stone walls.

Despite the numerous attempts to distract his thoughts away from what had happened during their last supper, James failed. He was harassed continuously by his thoughts concerning Jesus' betrayal. He was also troubled by what Jesus said about the bread before it was offered to him—the body? And by what Jesus said about the wine—the blood?

James shook his head, then glanced at Peter.

From Peter's sour expression, it was obvious that he was also troubled by what he had eaten, and by what he had to drink. But most of all, James assumed that Peter was more disturbed by what Jesus had said to him concerning his three time denial of him—of his Lord.

Peter could not hide the shame and the resentment that he felt; he kept in close step with Jesus even after they entered Gethsemane.

When they arrived at the center of the Garden, Jesus said, "*Pray that you will not fall into temptation.*"

Everyone was disturbed by this remark.

"Temptation about what?" James the younger wondered aloud. "Why is our Lord giving us this warning now?"

Nobody answered these questions.

Jesus stopped walking and turned to them. "*Sit here while I go over there and pray.*" Then he asked Peter, John, and James the elder to accompany him further into the Garden.

Many of those who were left behind sat on the ground feeling abandoned and insecure.

After the selected group reached the nearby upper-left section of the Garden, Jesus turned to the three and, to their surprise, confided something of his agony to them. "*The sorrow in my heart is so great that it almost crushes me.*" The earnest tone in Jesus' voice indicated his desire for them to maintain their attentiveness during this hour—the hour before his greatest tribulation, before he had to face his greatest pain alone; he ignored their blank stares. "*Stay here and watch.*"

The chosen three were as forlorn as those who had been left behind at the lower right section of the Garden.

Jesus strode to the western limit of the Garden where he knelt down, then threw himself on the ground.

They were all alarmed by the intensity of their Lord's prayer.

Thomas leaned toward James the younger. "Look at that."

"I see."

Thomas was dismayed. "I don't understand what he wants from me."

"To believe in him—I think."

"Yes, yes. But what does that mean?"

James did not know how else to answer this question. "Believe."

Thomas leveled his dark eyes at him. "That can't be all."

"I . . . I think it is." James adjusted his upper mantle. "So he says."

"Constantly. I know. He knows everything."

"Don't be cynical."

This reproach disarmed Thomas. "I'm . . . I'm feeling less than myself."

"I understand that."

Thomas clenched his teeth. "Every time Jesus is angry with me—"

"With us."

"Us. Yes. Our. Our moments of doubt have often disappointed him. Why do we lose our faith when he is not absolutely near us?"

"That's not true," said James.

"Look at us now." He pointed at their distant Lord. "And *we* are able to see and hear him."

James frowned, then conceded. "We *are* weak."

"Will you two shut up," Bartholomew complained. "I'm trying to pray."

"Listen to you," Thomas countered, then addressed James. "Listen to him."

"Well, let's try to pray," Bartholomew pleaded.

"Alright, alright," said Thomas.

James softened the annoyance between them. "May God help us."

And they prayed. For a while. Then they struggled with prayer. For a while. But the effects of the wine and the food, combined with their tiring journey across the valley, eventually triumphed over their intentions to pray fervently on their knees, like their Lord often did. But inactivity led to sitting, vagrancy led to reclining, and spiritual weakness led to slumber.

James descended into a deep dream about his difficult life as a young fisherman.

The nights were long and difficult on the Sea of Galilee and their catches were hard won.

Unlike the older men on the boats, the exhausting labor was often demoralizing for him after a long night of extreme exposure—especially if the night ended with a poor catch.

James was the weakest man aboard their fishing vessel. In fact, he was the weakest man among all the crews that worked aboard the nested boats that were tied up along their village's shoreline during the day. Despite that, he managed to be an able-bodied fisherman.

He was glad that he had the strength to work alongside men much bigger than himself; he wanted to be as tough as any of them. But in truth, he was not tough.

He pretended that he was eager to get underway; he wanted to embrace the difficulty of the occupation that he was born into. But in truth, he did not love his trade.

Preparing to get underway before nightfall was an all hands evolution concerning the necessary stowage of gear on-board the boat—food and clean water, nets and baskets, extra ropes and oars, torchlights and stone anchors; hooks, cords, and sinkers were also needed as well as buoys for the large dragnets. Anything missed would make their work harder and make the hours offshore feel longer.

Whoever forgot to bring on-board any part of a load-out that was assigned to him, the morning light and the welcomed sight of the shoreline could not come soon enough. The irritated boat-mates would make life miserable for that man—a misery that was often out of proportion to a crew's discomfort.

This misery was an experience that James wanted to avoid from happening again after he forgot to replenish their boat with the torches that were needed to attract fish to the surface, and needed to provide the light to work by—especially during a moonless night.

A fishing boat was a world lit by fire. Without torches lighting the boat's deck to see, the surrounding darkness could be so deep that it would slow down their work and, in some cases, the darkness could be so forbidding that it would become too dangerous to work.

On the night of his blunder, however, his boat-mates were determined to stay out on the lake—no matter the danger; they were determined not to return to their village without a catch—no matter how modest.

Hoarse grunts harassed him throughout that gloomy voyage. And guilt lessened his frequency at standing close by his boat-mates. To make matters worse, the sky was starless because of a heavy overcast, which further disoriented the crew—and made him feel lonelier. Even his eagerness to work harder at hauling in the meager catch in their nets did not reduce the amount of harassment by his boat-mates throughout this black and difficult night. After this experience, he was determined to find a way out.

James was amazed when he succeeded in convincing his boat-mates that he would be able to produce a good result from fishing ashore if he were permitted to do so.

He worked hard to achieve a successful outcome—a respectable catch worthy of their approval. It was independent work that could be employed at his own speed. And more importantly, he would not have to listen to the constant criticism by the older men. Also, being closer to the women gave him a special kind of stature that he appreciated. He was careful, however, not to take advantage of this minor position. Losing their warmth toward him would result in finding himself back on a boat. So he kept his commands in check and uttered his few requests in a respectful tone toward those sympathetic women, who voluntarily assisted him by sorting the fish that he caught—separating the clean from the unclean.

James was proud of his skill at casting his small net over the shallow water's edge. He was able to produce a broad spinning motion, which allowed the net to expand into a proper ring, before it fell onto the water's surface. The lead weights attached to the net's outer ring would pull the net to the bottom. And as it sank, the net's fine mesh would create a dome, which enclosed the fish. The true labor would begin, however, after he pulled the line closed that was attached to the net. Now the weight of the catch, entangled in the net, had to be hauled ashore.

Because it was exhausting work, he always appreciated whenever a boy from the village offered to help him. Understandably, he was especially careful not to criticize any boy's assistance; he kept his commands in check and his requests respectful, like he did with the women.

He liked the feel of the calf high water and the feel of the silt on the bottom of his feet. He liked knowing that he could sit and rest and drink water whenever he wanted to. He liked not having to answer to anybody. And he liked being able to stop work early enough to get a few hours of sleep before the boats returned at morning's first light. Like the others in the village, he would help the exhausted boatmen unload the catch and the gear.

The unloading and the sorting of fish was the first, and most important, task that needed to be accomplished. Then the nets had to be placed on the racks to dry, and later, repaired. The large water jars had to be refilled, new torches needed to be brought on-board, and numerous other things had to be done during the morning in preparation for the following night's voyage.

The last thing that the boatmen attended to was their personal care: a light meal, a bath, and a change into clean clothes. Then from midday toward the approach of dusk it was rest and sleep with a conscious disregard for their aches and pains. When they finally rousted themselves out of their beds, they were greeted by their women and children, and were rewarded with a large and beautiful meal.

They ate freshly cooked fish that had been caught from the night before while they discussed fishing techniques, hoping to improve the result of the next catch during the upcoming night. They also enjoyed plates of rice and bread, fig-cakes and nuts; satisfied their tastes with dishes of sauce and bowls of vegetable stew; and quenched their thirsts with flasks of wine and pitchers of milk. Yes, that was a—

Someone jabbed his right side. James opened his eyes when he felt a second jab and realized that it was a tender kick from—"God!"—Jesus stood over him with Peter at his side.

James sat up and rubbed his eyes like a child attempting to hide his embarrassment. He was not given time to apologize.

"*Why are you sleeping?*" Jesus asked. "*Get up, and pray that you will not fall into temptation.*"

James stood up feeling defeated. "Lord, I . . . I . . . ." His eyes shifted from Jesus to Peter, then downward toward the ground of his being in shame.

"You are not alone," said Matthew, as he sat up. He stifled a yawn. "I have also failed in prayer, like you."

James gazed at him. "Like me."

"All of us failed," Peter confessed. He indicated the others with a grand sweep of his right arm. "Look at us. There. And there. And over there—see? Look. There are also a few us who are not yet awake."

Thomas stood up and struggled to clear his muddled head. "Did I hear that we have all fallen asleep?"

"*All* of us," said Peter.

"*Enough!*" Jesus shouted. "*The hour has come! Look, the Son of Man is now handed over to the power of sinful men. Look, here is the man who is betraying me!*"

A mob of men invaded the Garden—many were armed with clubs. They were accompanied by Temple Guards, who were armed with swords.

James was surprised by their approach. Then he felt foolish; he had accepted the notion that they were safe when Jesus had decided to continue staying in Gethsemane. Foolish.

There were too many people who knew that they were spending their nights in this garden—praying and resting and sleeping.

Jesus must have been aware of this. He must have been.

The mob surrounded them.

There was no escape.

Nothing could be done.

Judas emerged from behind two Temple Guards, approached Jesus, and said, "*Rabbi*," then kissed him.

James was baffled by Jesus' lack of emotion.

"*Is it with a kiss, Judas, that you betray the Son of Man?*" Jesus asked.

During the momentary tableau that followed, Peter peered at James. "So that's what you were told. You *knew* it was Judas who would betray him."

James was equally caustic. "I knew *nothing.*"

Simon drew out his dagger in a panic and wielded it at the closest Temple Guard. This led to sudden chaos and random violence.

Everything became a blur to James.

Several disciples were assaulted. Others, including Simon, ran.

The mob scattered.

Jesus was arrested by the Guards.

Someone cut off a man's ear.

James dropped to his knees after receiving a blow to the back of his head. He hunched forward, then fell face down to the ground.

Jesus commanded, "*Put your sword back in its place, because all who take the . . . sword . . . will . . . die . . . by—*"

The growing darkness, accompanied by the deepening silence of unconsciousness, prevented James from hearing the rest of—

Chapter 3

It was raining when James regained consciousness.

He sat up.

Shallow pockmarked puddles surrounded him.

He was hurt and afraid and alone.

Lightning attacked the hostile terrain. Then a strange and ominous darkness enveloped the world. Everything felt dangerous.

He stood up.

"What kind of late spring storm is this?"

He trembled.

"Where is this fierce rain and wind coming from?"

He shivered.

James did not understand why he had not been arrested.

After taking his first unsteady step, he almost lost his balance.

He leaned into a half crouch to steady himself, then massaged his right temple with the heel of his hand to ease his excruciating headache.

Although he was confused, he knew he had to leave Gethsemane.

His next step was steadier. And so was the next step and the next and then—

He kept walking and walking for what seemed to be a very long time and . . . .

James did not remember leaving Gethsemane—and, he did not remember traveling across the Mount of Olives to the edge of the Kidron Valley.

The back of his eyes hurt.

After entering the Valley, he neither knew in what direction he had taken, nor understood how much time had passed.

He crouched into a standstill when a slash of lightning streaked across the sky. And when he bowed his head in response to another violent streak, he noticed a bug scampering along the surface of a pockmarked mud puddle beneath him. "Even you are frightened by this weather."

He dropped to one knee before he heard someone say, "Shut up."

James searched in the direction of the voice and discovered a ragged formation of men, who appeared as wary as he felt—he sensed the fear of Rome in their behavior.

When he was certain that the command had not been addressed to him, he stood up feeling relieved, then joined the formation even though its destination was unknown to him.

The rain stopped. The strange darkness persisted.

The grim procession veered past a small cluster of squat, mud-brick dwellings to avoid barking dogs.

As they approached a cattle-fold's gate, the leader of the formation was hailed by a sentry, who stood by its open entrance with two other brutish men.

Within the rectangular cattle-fold's enclosure, there was a menagerie of beasts comprised of oxen, asses, and camels that roamed freely within its rock-wall perimeter. Swine were segregated into one corner by a fence. There was also a long flat-roofed stable on the other side where horses could be seen occupying the stalls on the left side of the stable through one of its open doors.

When the formation's leader reached the three men standing by the gate, the tone of their laughter was so sinister sounding that James veered clear of the formation and walked away from the cattle-fold as fast as he could without causing too much alarm.

"What's wrong with him?" one of the brutish men asked.

"Who cares," said the other man. "He's afraid of something."

"He's afraid of us."

Cruel laughter burst forth from the gate-sentries.

"He probably should be."

More cruel laughter erupted from several members of the formation.

James scurried away from a danger that seemed equal to Rome's.

Darkness and peculiar weather persisted for an undetermined period of time as he continued to travel across unfamiliar terrain.

James touched the back of his head in response to a sudden sharp pain. He pressed the palm of his left hand against the wound and winced. "Damn." He stopped walking, blinked at his surroundings, then licked his dry lips.

He was disoriented. Time had stopped. He did not know what to do.

James dropped to his knees in misery. His torment continued to deepen within this menacing environment. "How does prayer work?"

Strange celestial occurrences from the firmament above, along with solitary points of light here and there, penetrated through the haze of this present climate.

"How does belief work?" someone asked.

This intruding voice disturbed him.

James looked over his left shoulder and thought he saw a figure. "Our Lord spoke directly to his Father."

"And he encouraged you to do the same," said the figure.

"Do *you*?" James challenged.

"*I pray.*"

"To the Father?"

"To my Lord, Jesus. Yes. And the Father."

James stood up. "You're confusing me."

"The Father. The Son. The Holy Spirit. Yes. Our Lord requires your belief."

"Jesus was often impatient with me."

"But you followed him."

"Because he chose me to do so," said James.

"And you have followed."

"I have stumbled in his direction is nearer to the truth," James confided.

"And by what means do you manage to continue this stumbling?"

James hesitated. "Through his grace?"

"That's right. You have encountered his grace many times."

James straightened his cloak. "How do you know that?"

"You have heard him speak to the Father. You have witnessed the Son addressing himself. You have experienced the presence of the Holy Spirit."

"You did not answer my question." He stepped toward the figure. "Who are you?"

James hurried toward the place where he thought the figure was standing, but there was nobody there.

"Where are you? Where did you go? What is this?"

He pressed his nervous right hand against the lower lip of his half-open mouth and wondered if that blow to his head had caused some strange damage to his mind.

"Have I been speaking to myself? God help me."

After running away from where he stood, James ran in several directions seeking a destination.

"God help me!"

He dropped to his knees again in a despair so deep that he lost his balance and fell forward.

James waited for the approach of death while on his hands and knees.

Death did not come. Life did not—wait . . . .

"Jerusalem."

He stood up.

"I must find my way to Jerusalem."

A first step was taken, followed by a second, then followed by another and, with each additional step, he regained his sense of self.

Chapter 4

When James reached the city's gate, he asked the wary gatekeeper if there had been others who had entered Jerusalem recently.

The gatekeeper did not answer him. Instead, he reached for one of his oil lamps, unhooked it from a lamp-stand, and placed its modest light between them.

The portly gatekeeper raised the lamp to eye level and concluded that this lost pilgrim was a harmless youth, who was innocently seeking information about his people before entering the city.

James squinted at the closely held light, then blinked his eyes before he expressed his concerns about the unnatural weather that was plaguing the region and making travel more difficult.

"Yes, yes," said the gatekeeper. "Those who have passed through my needle's eye recently have been troubled by the extremes that have been cast upon us from above." He lowered the lamp, then hooked it onto its lamp-stand. "I don't know what to make of it. Do you?"

"I have no idea what to make of anything."

The gatekeeper was amused by that answer. "Well said, young man."

"I was speaking plainly."

"And directly. Very good." The gatekeeper rubbed the right side of his pockmarked face with his left hand. "How were you separated from your people?"

"Separated?" James considered the question. "Yes. We were separated." He adjusted the front of his cloak. "The *how* is too long a story."

"Ah. Of course. Always too long." The gatekeeper approached the small wooden door built into the massive gate. "Separated from brothers? Or from brethren?"

James pressed his right fist into his left palm. "Both."

"Easy there, young man, easy. You will find them." The gatekeeper lifted the door's crossbeam off of two iron braces. "With God's help. You'll see." He set aside the crossbeam. "You will find them. Yes. You'll see."

"Yes." James peered at the ominous firmament above. "I'll see."

"Be careful." The nervous gatekeeper opened the small door. "People are behaving oddly under this . . . this abnormal sky. I swear, it's been hard for me to breathe in this heavy air."

James passed through the needle's eye without knowing where he was going.

He hurried along a dark street, tripped over the legs of a homeless man who was asleep nearby a wall, and stumbled to a halt. "I'm sorry."

The man did not respond to him.

James proceeded more carefully along the narrow thoroughfare, which stank of rotted refuse and of decaying human waste—a condition that afflicted the open-air in this lower region of Jerusalem.

An occasional dwelling emitted a feeble light through a second floor window that, at times, also framed a furtive silhouette.

A pack of aggressive dogs crossed the far end of the street.

Numerous scavenging mongrels could be heard barking and growling and fighting among each other beyond the intersection ahead.

James shuddered.

A long roll of thunder could be heard traveling across a distant terrain not far beyond the city's wall.

These strange weather conditions were having an abnormal effect upon every living creature—some were confused, others were dangerous.

James was lost in the many streets of dark Jerusalem, and frightened by the many threats of hidden beasts.

After avoiding numerous packs of dogs while traveling across this hostile city, he suddenly exhaled melancholy.

"How easily I have fallen. How quickly I have been reduced."

James discovered an unoccupied void underneath an outside stairway of a two story stone dwelling. He crouched toward the entrance and stepped inside of the sodden space. Then he sat on the moist ground and leaned against the structure's wall.

He trembled at the emptiness of it all. He shivered from the dampness and the cold, from his weakness and his fear.

Lifting his dirty upper mantle from his shoulders and raising it over the top of his head before bringing it down over his face to hide from reality did not provide him with comfort.

James licked his parched lips and wished he could find a well. A drink of fresh water would have been wonderful. But like a child, he was afraid to venture away from this safe place. And like a child, he had to be satisfied with the dry taste of uncertainty, and be content with the innocent veil of an upper mantle—his pathetic attempt to hide from reality.

He pressed his dirty mantle against his face feeling ashamed.

"You are lost. You have surrendered yourself to the poverty of cowardice."

James leaned toward the stairway's opening.

"Redemption is not possible for a man who is hiding from packs of wild beasts."

He fought against a terrible emptiness.

"Where are you, my Lord?"

A dog growled nearby.

James pulled his dirty mantle away from his face, lifted it over his head, and let it drop onto his shoulders. He blinked into the gloom.

Dogs ruled this world.

Chapter 5

James pressed his back against the damp wall of the stairway's void. He reached for his breath with difficulty. Fear and trembling had affected his senses, as well as his soul. He wished he was sitting near a charcoal fire so he could warm himself.

He slid the palm of his right hand across his chest and snagged his middle finger in a hole on the left side of his worn out cloak. The frayed edges of the hole was the result of wear rather than tear.

Until now, he had not noticed the condition of this garment.

He massaged his temples to ease his headache, then placed the palms of his hands on the ground to steady himself. But something crawled over the top of his left hand, which unnerved him.

"Damn."

James shook his left hand, then scratched the back of it with his right.

He leaned back against the wall again and wiped off the dirt and sand from the palms of both hands against his cloak.

"What have I become without Jesus' presence?"

Without Jesus he was nothing. Without Jesus—look at him now. This can't be. Had the last three years been an illusion?

"This is too dark. I can't pursue this."

James leaned away from the wall and peered into the gloom in an effort to escape from this impoverished condition, and from this madness that tormented him. He searched for any means of escape, for anything that would provide him with some comfort—there was none to be found. James closed his eyes and searched within himself until he discovered, suddenly, the forgotten comfort of his family—his lovely family.

Tension escaped his body. His headache eased. He breathed peacefully.

He missed his young wife and child, and hoped they were safe in Galilee where he had asked them to stay and not travel with him and Jesus and the others into the wide and unfriendly countryside of Judea—and then eventually into the formidable city of Jerusalem. It had been months since they left Galilee and he was glad that his wife was not facing the darkness that he was facing now.

He shifted his thoughts toward his very young son and managed to smile when he remembered that the boy was learning how to master the art of casting his small training net by the shoreline. He was a natural fisherman.

Like himself, his son was born into this profession. But unlike himself, his son was fond of the fishing trade. And for that, James was grateful. Because fishing was a hard and miserable occupation that he simply endured. Answering Jesus' call was a gift, and an escape from a world he was forced to like.

James inhaled a small measure of gratitude concerning his son, who looked forward to becoming a fisherman, and who did not need to be disciplined by his mother—a good woman.

There was comfort in knowing that his family was safe at home. He was determined to hold onto that illusion.

He touched his chest.

The loose threads of his worn out cloak were no illusion. The cold and the surrounding emptiness were no illusion. His internal doubts were . . . were real—as real as his thirst for water, as real as his desire for Jesus' presence. "Oh Lord, Lord, come back to me. Please. Come back to me."

A gruff voice startled him.

"Mangy dog!"

James opened his eyes.

The silhouette of a man appeared at the mouth of a dark alleyway across the street. The man stumbled, then fell down.

A dog growled. Another barked.

The night had too many eyes.

"You are nothing!" The man rolled onto his left side, gasped for air, then groaned. "Did you say something?"

A dog appeared and snapped at him.

"Did you say something?"

Another dog appeared and barked threateningly.

"Nothing!" He laughed. "You're nothing seems to have a lot to say."

Inner voices seemed to be tormenting this man. He was possessed.

The man rose to his knees and picked up a stone. "You mangy curs!" He threw the stone at one of the threatening dogs.

When the stone hit its mark, the dog yelped and danced in a stiff circle of pain.

In response to another hurled stone, the of dogs scattered and barked continuously as they scurried away.

James leaned toward the opening of the stairway's void after suddenly recognizing this man's voice. "Judas?"

The man cowered. "What?"

"Judas. It's me—James!"

Judas straightened up. "Is it truly you?" He threw another stone, then splashed across several puddles toward James, who crawled out of the stairway's void before Judas reached him.

James touched Judas's right shoulder. "Yes."

"No." Judas pressed his forehead against James's left shoulder and sobbed. "I am an illusion. Everything is an illusion—everything is nothing. Do you understand?"

Dogs continued to bark in the distance.

"I am too confused about what you had to do, to understand anything," said James. "I am miserable over what has happened."

"You are?" Judas eyes widened with the glimmer of a madman. "Is there sympathy in that misery? Is there?"

Judas pushed himself away from James. "My God, my God, why has he forsaken me?"

"I know what the Lord said to you during our last supper." James approached Judas and placed his right hand upon his left shoulder. "You're not forsaken."

"Did you see his eyes?" He brushed James's hand away. "I can't feel our Lord's presence."

"Judas." The sympathetic tone in his voice was flat and colorless. James did not know how to comfort him. "Judas."

"My God, my God—"

"We cannot be forsaken. We must not be. Please."

Judas moaned. "I am lost." He grabbed the front of James's cloak.

James could not deflect Judas from his anguish, could not protect him from his illusions, and could not repair his broken faith. "Look at me. I'm in hiding too."

Judas released James's cloak, then leaned against the outside stairway of the two story dwelling. "In hiding? Oh. I'd give anything if I could be in hiding." He bit his lower lip. "Did you see our Lord's eyes in the Garden when I kissed him?"

"No," said James. "No. The arrest happened too fast."

"You didn't." Judas was disappointed. "I cannot hide from those eyes. Where is the Kingdom of God now?"

"Jesus understood your burden. I heard it in his voice when he told me about the why, and the what, you had to do—"

"Throughout all time." Judas moaned.

"This was not your choice."

"That's right." A flicker of hope illuminated Judas's eyes. "That's right!"

"I would have helped you if—"

"Don't, lie to me!" Judas's madness intensified suddenly. "You're glad that it wasn't you. Admit it! Say it!"

"I won't!"

"Don't insult me!" Judas grabbed the front of James's cloak again and shook him.. "You're glad, I say—glad that it wasn't you!"

"Let me go!"

"Say it!" Judas released the cloak before he struck James. The blow to the left temple was so forceful that James was unconscious before he fell upon the ground.

Chapter 6

Jerusalem was awake when James opened his eyes and blinked repeatedly at the daylight—the strange gloom was gone.

He sat up and pressed his left hand against his temple. "God help me."

His excruciating headache forced him to lean forward in an effort to find relief. He took a deep breath.

"Judas."

Then he exhaled.

"Poor Judas."

He leaned toward his right side to counter a sickening sensation of dizziness, and kept still to prevent himself from vomiting. Then he maneuvered onto his knees and oriented himself before he stood up.

James supported himself against a wall until he was certain that he had gained enough stability to walk. Then he pushed himself away from the wall and took a clumsy step that planted him, briefly, into a standstill. He waited several moments until he felt confident enough to travel along the busy thoroughfare. He lost his confidence, however, when he stepped into a pothole of wet refuse and lost his balance—he did not fall.

"Damn."

He almost lost his right sandal when he pulled his foot out of the stinking muck.

"What a mess."

James limped away from the pothole and sat on the ground. He pulled off the sandal, shook it out, then slipped it back on.

"Alright. I'm alright. I must keep moving."

He stood up, took a deep breath, then continued to plod aimlessly along the crowded thoroughfare.

Venders were busy selling their merchandise; women were occupied with their domestic tasks; craftsmen were working in their open-air shops.

The complex maze of dwellings and streets and strange structures in lower Jerusalem made him feel nervous and enclosed and suspicious toward this crowded way of life.

He was overwhelmed by the extent of the surrounding activity that assaulted his senses and that forced him to have multiple impressions about city life; impressions that produced conflicting and resentful thoughts about these harried inhabitants.

He was wary of these city people because, to his astonishment, he had discovered recently that the crowds listening to Jesus outside the walls of this city were primarily composed of these Jerusalem dwellers, who felt superior to him—James the younger, a mere fisherman. And to his increased astonishment, he had discovered that those who lived here in this lower section of Jerusalem, also behaved as if they were superior to the people living in the surrounding countryside, even though they themselves were working class people—skilled and unskilled laborers, struggling shopkeepers, potters, brick makers, butchers, cheese makers, copper smiths, hewers of stone, metal workers, weavers, barbers, shoemakers, bakers, cooks, servants, wailers, midwives—all.

He pouted.

Why would they feel superior to those who worked in the countryside like farmers, shepherds, fishermen, herdsmen, tanners, gardeners, fullers of cloth, bee keepers—all.

He pursed his lips, It seemed reasonable, however, to understand the superior attitudes of those who generally lived in upper Jerusalem—the bankers, builders, innkeepers, rich merchants, physicians, teachers, rabbis, priests, pharisees—yes. They were the learned men who owned most of the city and who determined what was good for the people.

James grimaced.

Why should this attitude exist in any form?

Those who lived in the countryside were certainly smart enough to live their lives in a manner that they chose to, since they earned it and paid their way—as well as provided most of the food and much of the necessary goods needed to sustain life. Without them, there would not be a Jerusalem. There would not be *any* city.

James was perplexed. No. Irritated. No. He was angry, because these thoughts reminded him of how much he suddenly missed living in his fishing village, and missed working on the lake—despite his dislike for the trade.

He smiled at this contradiction.

Then again, recalling his fishing life also made him appreciate the privilege of wandering and preaching in Galilee and in Judea with Jesus; appreciate the privilege of living the kind of life that no longer brought calluses to his hands.

He frowned.

Then again, he no longer felt the physical satisfaction of exhaustion, after a demanding voyage, which preceded a well earned deep and satisfying sleep—accompanied by the warmth of his wife during the early hours.

He smiled again.

Yes. He had to admit that he missed the special openness of his fishing village by the Sea of Galilee. It was a place of good and honest work that provided fish for the nearby villages and towns, as well as for the large city of Capernaum to the north.

Irritation caught hold of him again as he continued his aimless journey through this lower city, and as he continued to wrestle with his contentious thoughts.

Good and honest work from those who toiled on the land and upon the sea was necessary to these people living in Jerusalem. And yet, he sensed from these permanent city dwellers a distrust toward him and toward anybody who looked and behaved as if they labored on the land or on the sea.

He scowled.

He resented the city attitude and dismissal by these so-called elites, who had forgotten where their food came from. He was comforted, however, that it was the common people like himself, who listened and believed and followed the Lord—they were not dismissed by Jesus.

Our Lord was not really real through the eyes of city dwellers. They couldn't—no—wouldn't understand or accept him. No! They had to arrest him. God help us. They know not what they have done.

"Lord. Lord. Where is my Lord?" he exclaimed, in response to his whirling thoughts.

"Arrested. Condemned. Crucified," someone answered.

James stopped walking and turned toward—toward a figure, who stood on the other side of the thoroughfare.

There was something familiar about him. His voice, perhaps?

The lower half of the figure's countenance was veiled by an upper mantle.

"Where did you come from?"

"Over there." The veiled figure pointed at the intersection to his left. "I recognized you."

"Over where?" James gazed at the intersection expecting to discover—"Wait. Condemned? Crucified?" He peered at the figure. "I know he was arrested, but . . . but did I hear you say condemned and crucified?"

"Yes. And died."

"Died." James was devastated by this news. "When?"

The veiled figure crossed the thoroughfare. "*When* that storm assaulted the world."

James had difficulty recovering from the terrible news concerning his Lord's death. "That storm . . ."

"Announced his acceptance of death."

" . . . assaulted the world."

"A world that was covered, suddenly, by the many hours of unnatural darkness."

"Unnatural."

"A world that was immersed, suddenly, by the heavy weight of immeasurable grief."

"Grief?" With immense effort, James exhaled his stupor. "Grief."

"Most people were frightened."

"I was most people."

The veiled figure drew closer to James. "Then our Lord was taken down from the wood before the Sabbath."

"Taken down." James shuddered.

"According to the Law."

"According to—" James paused during a sideways glance at this curious figure. "Do I know you?"

"You should."

"But I don't."

"Be not afraid. I am with the Lord, Jesus."

James's doubt was in harmony with his distrust. "You are?"

"Yes. I know. I am not one of the privileged twelve."

"Not so privileged. Look at me. I'm nothing."

"All is nothing without him."

"I should know that." James stepped back from the figure and accidentally collided with a pedestrian. "I'm sorry."

The pedestrian acknowledged him with a nod, then proceeded toward his destination. James remained where he stood. "I should know that."

"You are one of the twelve. Yes."

James ignored the condescension. "Where are the others?"

"Where are you?"

James adjusted his upper mantle, which was draped over his shoulders, as he searched for an answer. "I don't know."

"I will tell you this: your brethren disciples abandoned the Lord."

James side stepped another approaching pedestrian. "Why don't I know you? What is your name?"

"I will not give you a name."

"But—"

"I had no name when you were among the twelve. I will have no name now. You look hungry and thirsty. Come with me."

James hesitated.

"Come. Please."

James followed the figure to an establishment that was covered by a large canopy held aloft by four poles. Numerous mats carpeted the ground inside.

They approached the transaction table and waited for the owner of the establishment to join them.

"What would you like to eat? You should be hungry."

"I am." James caught sight of the approaching merchant and addressed him as soon as he stepped behind the transaction table. "Do you have bread, cheese, and milk?"

"Of course I do. One moment please."

They did not have to wait long.

The merchant set the items on the table, then pointed toward the left side of the establishment. "You can sit over there and eat. Those cups on that corner mat are yours to drink from."

"Thank you." James cradled the bread and cheese against his chest with his left arm and picked up the milk pitcher by its narrow neck with his right hand.

They approached the designated corner and sat down opposite each other.

James poured milk into two cups, picked up one, and drank half the milk. Then he ate without a word of blessing until the silence of the veiled figure began to annoy him.

He burped.

"Crucified." James finished drinking the milk that was left in his cup.

"And taken down from the wood after he died on Golgotha."

James set the empty cup on the mat. "Golgotha." The flat tone of his voice reflected his dour disposition.

"It is located that way. Toward the western wall. Anyone can direct you should you get lost while going there."

"Should I get lost?"

"Never mind that."

James brushed his dark brown beard with the finger-tips of his right hand. "So, then, you were there?"

"In spirit. Yes."

"Were *any* of us . . . ." James clenched his teeth. "Were any of my . . . my brethren disciples with him?"

"There was *one*."

"Only one?"

"Yes. It was John. He stood with the women."

"Ah. The women," said James. "So the women *were* there."

"Yes. And John wept like one, as he cowered among them."

"Our Lord told us that this would happen," said James.

"You mean, John's behavior."

"I mean—our, *my* cowardly behavior." James pressed the palm of his left hand against his forehead. "I am a coward. Like the others. All of us fled like children during his arrest. No. Worse. We behaved like frightened dogs." He lowered his hand onto his lap. "Our Lord was being kind to us when he simply told us that we would abandon him."

"And you refused to believe what Jesus foretold."

"Of course, I refused to believed that. All of us refused. And all of us denied openly that we would not commit such a terrible act." James shifted nervously from side to side on the mat. "You had to have been there to truly understand our refusal."

"Oh. I see."

"I'm sorry. I did not intend to offend you."

"You didn't."

James ate a piece of bread. "Yes, I was one of the twelve, but I am also a stupid man—a man who never understood our Lord even after all the time I spent with him."

"I have been too hard on you. Forgive me."

"You've done nothing against me to forgive. Believe me. If anything, it is I who should be forgiven."

"The Lord loves us. That's all you need to know."

James frowned. "Love can be lost in a moment."

"He said he would always love you."

"Love. He spoke too much of love."

"You mystify me," said the veiled figure. "You speak like a stranger to—"

"My self. Yes. I don't know what this love is about."

"How can you speak in this manner after all the time you have spent with the Lord?"

"I'll speak any way I like."

"Interesting. You seem to have certainty about this, even though you are uncertain about everything else."

"I know nothing." James scowled. "*Love.* What is it, if it can be suddenly lost?"

"Love can never be lost."

"It can be lost, I said!"

"You are speaking nonsense."

"Where is this love now?" James challenged. "How do I touch it? How do I touch him?"

"You are the one who has been suddenly lost. Not love."

James was unable to respond to that.

"*His* love is real."

"And his love is eternal—I know, I know." James waved his hands to further express his exasperation. "I know. I have heard it all."

"You are supposed to know that he is always present."

James exhaled bewilderment. "I am not *feeling* it."

"Calm yourself and try to remember: God is always present."

"Who are you?" James demanded. "How have you acquired this faith?"

"God is present."

"God *is* present. I agree. But love is not."

"You have not understood the truth in his Good News."

"Ah, the wisdom in the Good News," James announced facetiously. "Yes. The truth in his Good News."

"You must have understood it when the Lord sent you out into the countryside and into the villages to speak of this truth. You were one of the twelve and yet—wait. Why do you appear so perplexed right now? Didn't you understand what you were saying? Didn't you understand anything about what the Lord taught you?"

"I told you I never understood our Lord. Remember? I've been a mimic. I did not know what I was talking about."

"And apparently, you continue not to know."

James laughed. "You think that hurts me?"

"There was no bitterness in your voice when you spoke the truth in the villages."

"The truth, the truth. What is truth?" James sighed. "I am sick of trying to understand this truth."

"You can't be the one to understand it."

"I can do—"

"Nothing. You've proven that to yourself. And yet, you were speaking *His* truth in the villages. And in the countryside, you, yourself, listened to the Lord speak repeatedly about the Good News."

James sighed. "I have used up all the faith I have listening to, and speaking about, *the Good News*. I admit, I understood from a distance. And I spoke from within a cloud. I don't know myself."

"You'll feel better after you finish eating your food. You'll see."

James forced himself to eat. "I want to understand something."

"You will."

"But I have been in our Lord's presence for three years and, look at me, I haven't learned anything."

"I know that. I have always been at his side."

"I don't understand that," said James. "I have never seen you."

"It's not possible to see through one's internal darkness."

"What do you know about that darkness?" James demanded.

"The struggle against its emptiness influences most behavior."

James glanced at their cups. "Don't you ever struggle against that darkness within?" His cup was empty, the other cup was full of untouched milk. "Don't lie to me."

"Not in our Lord's presence."

"What about now?" James pressed.

"He is always present. Remember? Don't lose faith in him."

"That's not an answer. Everyone struggles against the darkness of confusion and the emptiness of doubt and—"

"You're thinking too hard. Thinking does not give comfort."

"What I wouldn't do for an hour of that comfort," James concluded.

"You can't do it."

"There it is, once again. I don't understand that."

"You don't have to understand the will of the Lord— who is present."

"He is dead," James asserted. "You said so yourself."

"You're thinking again. Yes. He was crucified. To end death."

"What does that mean?"

"To end death is to invite you into the Kingdom of God."

James was exasperated. "The Kingdom of God. The Kingdom of God! I can't get that into my head."

"That won't happen."

"Then what will? What is God's will?"

"You will have to receive that will from the Lord. His will cannot be attained. It must be *given* to you."

"Receive his will." James placed his hands on the floor mat behind him and leaned back against his outstretched arms for support. "It must be given?"

"That's right. It can't be attained."

"I'm not sure I can understand that."

"The Lord's presence has given you meaning even though you don't know it yet."

"His presence?" James laughed. "His presence has simply awakened me to . . . ."

"To what? If not to the Kingdom."

"To what."

"You *are* in trouble right now. But the light will come. You'll see." A long silence followed. "Remember. Jesus."

"Remember," said James. "Yes."

"This sorrow of yours will pass."

"What is your name?"

"Close your eyes and try to relax for a moment. Go on. Close your eyes."

James closed his eyes hoping that if he cooperated with whomever this was, that it would help him unlock some of his uncertainty.

When he opened his eyes, the veiled figure had vanished.

He stood up, searched the establishment, then stepped outside. "Gone? Gone." He turned toward the entrance of the establishment and approached the merchant, who was standing behind the transaction table. "The one who came in here with me. Where did he go?"

The merchant was perplexed. "Where did who go?"

"The one who sat with me over there?"

"Over there, you say?"

"Yes, yes."

"There was no one sitting with you."

"That's impossible," said James. "Are you sure? He sat over there and . . . and—alright. *He's* the one who bought the bread and cheese and milk."

"I thought *you* were the one who placed the money right here, on my table, while I was filling your pitcher with milk."

James was dismayed. "The money."

The merchant grew sullen. "I suppose you want change. Well there's—"

"No. No." James did not know what else to say. He turned away from the annoyed merchant, stepped into the street, and scanned the area.

The veiled figure had vanished.

It suddenly occurred to him that this unidentified being did not eat any food or drink any milk.

He studied the length of the thoroughfare in both directions. "No sign."

James took several steps away from where he stood in an effort to leave behind his confusion; he almost collided with a man who was riding on an ass instead.

He approached a narrow alleyway and posted himself near its entrance to avoid the thoroughfare's steady traffic.

"Crucified. Died. And taken down."

He trembled in response to what he knew he had to do.

"Golgotha. I must go there."

He abandoned the alleyway's entrance, took several steps toward this necessary destination, then stopped.

"My Lord, my Lord. Please give me courage. Please."

Chapter 7

Golgotha, Gulgulta, Gulgoleth, Calvarius—the Greek, the Aramaic, the Hebrew, and the Latin names for the place of the skull: a cranial-shaped rocky elevation located outside of Jerusalem near its western wall, and located close to several main roads that led to various cities and towns such as Caesarea and Joppa, Bethlehem and Hebron.

The gray sky managed to generate enough light to pass through the thick atmosphere and illuminate the overcast souls on the mound.

Most of those who stood on Golgotha's foothills were burdened by their sorrow over what had happened to Jesus of Nazareth.

Two Roman Auxiliary Legionnaires had been posted on this hill to maintain order.

One of these Legionnaires was sitting on a flat rock with his helmet on his lap—his shield was lying on the ground beside him with his seven-foot pilum resting upon it. The other Legionnaire stood guard at some distance from the three crosses. He was fully assembled—helmet set low on his brow, shield held against his left side, and pilum anchored vertically to the ground with his right hand.

Vultures circled high above their helpless prey.

Ravens waited, here and there, upon jagged rocks.

No scrubs. No grass. No chickweed. No vegetation, managed to push its way through the hard rock surface of its high ground or through the softer surface of its foothills. It was as if all plant life had deliberately abandoned this forlorn place of execution and death; a place where many of the rocks had a sharp edge to them, which threatened harm to any creature that chose to tramp carelessly upon this ground.

Despite the recent storm, this insignificant place felt arid.

James stood on its perimeter feeling overwhelmed by the malevolence that governed this place.

With his left hand, he pulled back the top of his upper mantle and let it fall onto his shoulders. Then he untied the back of his head-wrap that was beginning to loosen, unfurled the length of the bleached linen, and wiped his face with it. After scratching his right temple through his dark-brown hair, he shook out the long strip of cloth and wrapped it securely around his head. He caught the musty scent of wet wool as he readjusted his mantle upon his shoulders.

This minor attention to his appearance did not calm his overburdened mind, and did not reveal the depth of his uncertainty to any of the nearby women.

When he summoned the courage to confront the crosses, despondent utterances escaped from his hidden thoughts.

"Three. One empty. My Lord's. Injustice. My God. Abandoned."

James turned away in despair and approached a group of women, who gave him permission to stand alongside them. He felt unworthy to be included in their sorrow.

The women endured the discomfort of their sodden tunics—a consequence of that long and gloomy storm, which occurred after Jesus' death. Feminine beauty and dignity managed to rise above the poverty of their dress. In fact, the homeliness of their attire amplified those who were beautiful, and emphasized the dignity of those who were elderly.

Despite this abundant presence of feminine grace, however, the truth of poverty brought attention to the threadbare state of those who were crippled or diseased, homeless and abused.

The overall condition of their garments varied from rough and heavy wool, to delicate and lighter worn-out linen, which had been passed down to them from their masters or from their wealthy family members. Cloth, instead of leather, served as belts to hold their full length tunics close to their bodies. Adornments were rare.

Their wet upper mantles, being used as veils, were in various states of disrepair—all, hung soddenly upon their heads, necks, and shoulders. The faces of many girls, maidservants, and those of the very low class, however, were not veiled. Instead, they wore their mantles like shawls in defiance of this unjust execution. They would not hide their disapproval or their long braided hair. Their grief was exposed for anyone to see.

All of these women were either Judeans or Galileans. There were no rich foreigners among them, who would have worn silk and would have displayed precious stones or fancy embroidery on their clothes.

James gathered enough courage to address the stalwart woman standing beside him. "What happened to our Lord?"

"In the end," she answered, "when Jesus was dying, up there, in that most desperate place, he prayed."

James exhaled sorrow. "He always prayed whenever . . . ." He gazed at the empty cross. "He always sought high ground to pray."

"High ground," was her barren response beneath her dark-brown eyes. She examined the terrain. "Not so high."

He encouraged her to share what else she had witnessed. "He prayed?"

"For others."

"Of course." Tears threatened to escape from the interior corners of his eyes.

"*And* for himself," she added. "Everybody needs God."

He indicated the empty cross. "Where is God now?"

She spoke as if she did not hear his question. "Then our Lord took a final breath and exhaled the world."

James was unable to follow her last statement. He studied each of the three crosses without knowing what he was expecting to discover.

The unoccupied cross at the center was impaled into the hard and unforgiving ground like the other two crosses, which where occupied by broken men.

He glanced at the man to his left, then at the one to his right. They had been left hanging on the wood to be torn and eaten by the wolves this coming night; then torn by the carrion birds above and pecked by the awaiting ravens on the following morning. One of the men appeared to be dead; the other one was alive and, unfortunately, it appeared as if he was going to be strong enough to suffer the onslaught of those wolves this coming night.

James shuddered at that grim thought. "Rome."

The woman he had questioned responded to his revulsion at the condition of these men. "Thankfully, our Lord was taken down to be washed and anointed, then wrapped and buried before Sabbath's arrival."

"Then why do you, and the others, continue to remain here?"

"Those two men need prayer." She peered at the beasts of prey flying above. "And protection." She leveled her gaze at him. "Besides, there's nowhere to go."

James crossed his arms over his chest. "I understand." Then he turned to the man who occupied the cross on his left. "He's so young."

"Yes. And a Greek. He died a while ago. God will have mercy on him."

"How do you know that?"

"He was told, that today, he would be in paradise with him."

"With whom?"

"With our Lord, Jesus."

"I see." James felt foolish. "Jesus. He was told?"

"Yes," she answered, then added, "The boy asked our Lord to remember him when he came into his Kingdom."

James lowered his arms to his side. "His Kingdom. Paradise." He turned to the occupied cross on his right. "And this other man?"

"He is a Judean—though, a nonobservant brute, and an unrepentant professional criminal." She sighed. "They *were* thieves—both of them." The woman faced the empty cross, knelt on the ground, and prayed aloud for redemption, and for the increase of sanctification.

A long time passed before a frail and crippled woman, who was leaning on a cane, felt the need to announce, "The Nazarene is dead. Jesus is dead."

Several women wailed in response.

Then verbal outbursts poured forth from numerous women:

"Is this the end?" She was young. A slash of lightning cut the sky above her.

"My God. Who was that man?" She was old. A gust of wind blew through her.

"That was no man." She was pregnant. A distant roll of thunder rumbled underneath her.

"He was the Messiah." She was sick.

"What good is a dead Messiah?" She was depressed.

"God abandoned him." She was a girl.

"Man betrayed him." She was adolescent.

"He was the Son of Man." She was a mother.

"He was the Son of God," a grandmother said, with a tone of finality in her voice.

James stared at the empty cross, then raised his arms toward it to reveal his sorrow and express his desire to be forgiven.

When he heard the approach of another threatening storm, it frightened his primitive being.

He opened his extended hands and tried to reach into the Kingdom of God.

Wind. Distant thunder and lightning. Fear and trembling. No rain.

The Legionnaire sentries remained unaffected by the changing conditions of the weather, and by the rambling lamentations of the women.

PART II

MATTHEW THE PUBLICAN

Chapter 8

"*I tell you the truth*," said Jesus, "*one of you is going to betray me.*"

The men at the supper table were traumatized.

"Surely you don't mean me," Andrew whispered.

"Nor me—"

"Or me."

"I'm innocent."

Their agitated whispers continued at the table despite Matthew's strong-willed declaration.

"This is outrageous!"

Their resentment deepened underneath the increase of their babble.

John stood up and insisted that he was also innocent.

In the midst of this chaos, Matthew saw Peter lean close to James the younger, which resulted in an intense verbal exchange between them.

James pushed himself away from Peter as he wiped his nervous lips with the back of his left hand. Reluctantly, he leaned toward Jesus and spoke to him.

James was astounded by what the Lord whispered into his left ear. And before James could fully respond to what he heard, Peter interrupted him by grabbing his forearm.

Peter wrenched James away from the Lord and pressed him into another intense verbal exchange.

James recoiled from whatever it was that Peter said to him.

Their contentious exchanges disturbed Matthew.

The denials at the table persisted. The resentments heightened. With a different group of men, violence would have erupted.

Matthew pressed his hands together, rested them against the edge of the table, and recollected who he had been before he was chosen by his Lord three years ago to be here with eleven other imperfect men.

As his thoughts unfurled within him, he felt less anxious.

When Matthew was called upon to follow Jesus, he had more money and education than the other disciples; he had been a rich publican, and they had been poor fishermen. This made him an outsider whose hands had always been soft, unlike theirs, which had grown soft. And although he was not as physically powerful as these men, his skillfulness as a bodyguard was equal to theirs.

The work of a publican, a tax collector and a customs gatherer for the Romans, did not require manual labor—but it was an equally difficult and dangerous occupation. The difficulty of the trade was not the ability to determine the amount of tax money that he had to demand for Rome, but how much more he could overcharge and keep for himself without being caught or legally challenged. The danger in this trade involved the frequent expression of scorn and loathing, which was often a prelude to an earnest dagger assault by a desperate peasant farmer facing homelessness and starvation.

No one was more detested in Jewish society than a tax collector working for Rome. He was considered a traitor who was not welcomed in the synagogues; a traitor who sold his soul to Rome for money. In doing so, Matthew had lost his moral center, his conscience, and his faith— until Jesus.

Now, his fine linen tunic and upper mantle had become faded, threadbare, and repair worn. The soles of his leather sandals were thin, and the leather strap around his waist had several cracks. But even though he had given up his wealth, he had managed to maintain his well groomed beard, mustache, and shoulder length hair as he followed Jesus to . . . to this.

Suddenly, Jesus silenced everyone by raising his right hand, then tore off a piece of bread from an untouched loaf. *"It will be one of you twelve, one who dips his bread in the dish with me. The Son of Man will die as the Scriptures say he will—"*

And, because Matthew was so overwhelmed by the tension of the others and so preoccupied by his quest for composure, he vaguely heard the remainder of what Jesus said. His eyes kept darting from one strained face to another until Judas broke his spell by rising from the table and saying, "Surely you don't mean me, Rabbi."

"So you say." Jesus gave him the piece of bread. *"Hurry and do what you must."*

Judas dipped the bread into a dish of sauce and ate it. Then he drank all the wine in Jesus' cup before he left the room.

Despite his self absorption, Matthew realized that Judas was more deeply disturbed by Jesus' declaration than anybody else at the table.

Matthew was unable to consider this matter further, however, because he was captivated by his Lord's solemn ritual concerning the blessing of the bread and the blessing of the wine. Then he was mystified by this sacred food that he was given to eat, and equally mystified by this sacred wine that he was given to drink.

Matthew continued to be captivated by the rite that his Lord was establishing by offering each man a share of this blessed bread and a share of this blessed wine, which had become a sacrament of—

His body? His blood? God's covenant?

Amid his reflection concerning this mystery, Matthew was startled when Peter rose abruptly, pounded the table with the heels of his fists, and cried, "I will never leave you even if all the rest do!"

What had he missed?

Matthew's distorted grin indicated his bewilderment to James when they glanced simultaneously at each other.

"*I tell you this, Peter*," Jesus answered, "*the cock will not crow today until you have said three times that you do not know me.*"

"I will never say I do not know you even if I have to die with you!" Peter shouted. He began pounding the table again and encouraged the others to do the same, which they did.

Matthew pounded the table not because he supported Peter's personal cause of resentment, but because he did not clearly understand what he had witnessed, and experienced, during this supper with his Lord, Jesus. Pounding the table was as good a method as any to conceal his puzzlement concerning this body and this blood of the Lord, which had been given—for him to eat, and to drink.

"God help me to understand this," said Matthew, amid the clamor of men who were not listening to each other. "God help us all."

Chapter 9

During the journey across the Kidron Valley to reach the Garden of Gethsemane, Matthew maneuvered alongside James the younger. "Are you alright?"

James would not respond.

"What did Peter say to you at our supper table?"

James conveyed his refusal to answer the question with a dismissive hand gesture, accompanied by a pair of evasive eyes.

Matthew was sympathetic to his reticence. He did not press him further.

When they reached the Mount of Olives, Matthew waited after they passed by several groves and entered the Garden before he felt able to express his understanding to James. But before he had a chance to speak, Jesus unexpectedly cautioned them.

"*Pray that you will not fall into temptation.*"

Matthew was perplexed by this statement. He was also surprised that Peter did not ask Jesus to clarify his warning.

When they approached the center of the Garden, Jesus stopped walking, turned to them, and said, "*Sit here while I go over there and pray."* Then he beckoned Peter, John, and James the elder to accompany him further into the Garden.

At first, Matthew was crestfallen. But his disappointment softened when he saw Jesus address the chosen three once they arrived at the upper left region of the Garden, then abandoned them. The three were dumbfounded by what was said to them.

When Jesus reached the western corner of the Garden, he took several short steps to his left in a tight circle, came to a stop, and looked up at the sky before he dropped to his knees. The prayer that followed became so fervent that Jesus threw himself on the ground.

Matthew did not express his concern about the extreme agony that he was witnessing even after several of his brethren indicated their distress about the intensity of Jesus' prayer.

In an attempt to imitate his Lord, Matthew went to his knees and applied himself to earnest prayer; his brethren knelt down in prayer as well. However, as time passed, their kneeling evolved into sitting and sitting evolved into reclining with a genuine intent to continue their prayers. But their inactivity, accompanied by their fatigue and the aftereffects of too much food and wine, led them into a spiritual repose, which evolved into a deep slumber.

For Matthew, this slumber came to an abrupt end when someone nudged his left shoulder. He sat up and rubbed his eyes.

"Wake up." Andrew was kneeling beside him. "We have acted like fools once again. Wake up."

Matthew hastened to his feet and caught sight of Peter standing over James the younger.

"Yes, that's right." Andrew stood up. "We have all failed. Even Peter has confessed to that."

As the others shook off their slumber, a chorus of excuses and apologies erupted from their—

"*Enough!*" said Jesus. "*The hour has come! Look, the Son of Man is now handed over to the power of sinful men. Look, here is the man who is betraying me!*"

A mob of angry men, escorted by Temple Guards, invaded the Garden.

The disciples were paralyzed with fear.

Matthew was horrified when he discovered that it was Judas who was leading this rabble.

Their Lord remained calm and reserved and courageous.

Judas stepped forward.

Jesus was kissed.

Judas was cold-hearted.

Matthew was sickened.

James the younger was terrified.

Jesus was arrested.

Thomas was assaulted.

Simon drew out his dagger.

Men shouted.

Disciples scattered.

Chapter 10

Disorientation ruled Matthew's reason to such an extreme that he ran out of the Garden and collided into a tall tree stump. He fell to the ground gasping for air.

The menacing threat of his pursuers, however, urged him to recover his breath and rise to his knees. When he heard voices, the will to survive brought him to his feet.

An unrecognizable cry in the distance provoked him to jog through several groves to maximize his concealment during his escape from the Mount of Olives. When he reached the eastern edge of the relatively barren Kidron Valley, he increased his jog to a run toward a thicket of willow bushes in the distance that seemed to be high and dense enough to conceal him.

He was exhausted by the time he reached the thicket, but he was satisfied with the safe harbor that it offered. He entered the refuge, crouched inside of it, and listened.

The relentless progress of dusk toward the approach of nightfall deepened the hard silence.

Matthew dropped to his knees feeling empty. Nothing stood between his belief and his cowardice.

He sat down, then rolled onto his left side. He was ashamed of his behavior.

"Forgive me, Lord. My Lord, Jesus. I have abandoned you. And now . . . now I, am in hiding. And now I, am in disgrace."

Matthew rolled onto his chest and pressed his forehead against the dirt.

"I understand nothing. Nothing!"

He dug the fingers of his outstretched hands into the dirt.

"I have been reduced to this cowardly behavior."

Upon hearing the aggressive hooves of Legionnaire cavalry-horses galloping across the distant terrain, Matthew pushed his chest off the ground with his arms, sat back on his knees, and peered over the thicket to see where they were going.

He inhaled.

Matthew was relieved when he discovered that the menacing cavalry, with their torch-lights held high against the darkness, were moving away from him.

He exhaled.

An ugly thought assaulted him.

If Jesus was truly the Messiah, why did he allow himself to be arrested? And if Jesus was . . . .

Matthew covered his face with the palms of his hands and trembled.

There were too many feelings at war within him.

Remorse and fear. Anguish and guilt. Discomfort and doubt.

Chapter 11

The night had been long and cold.

Matthew sat up. He ached all over.

Daybreak allowed him to peer across the hostile landscape. The remains of a diminished wind persisted in polishing that hard landscape and bend it to its will.

He coughed and sniffed and wiped his wet nostrils with the back of his left hand, then stood up.

He stepped out of the thicket and stretched his back as he studied the terrain and debated with himself about whether he should go into the city or not.

There were so many enemies in Jerusalem that it was hard to decide where to go in order to find someone who could be trusted.

Matthew feared the gatekeepers and the Legionnaires and the Temple Guards and—he cleared his throat.

"You need to get control of yourself and start acting like a man, damn you. You need to go to Jerusalem."

He stepped toward this destination with determination and traveled slowly across the Kidron Valley. And as he approached the city's eastern wall, a strange and palpable darkness descended upon the earth and extinguished the daylight.

A storm broke through the firmament above and attacked the world with a fierce and driving rain, accompanied by dangerous lightning and threatening thunder.

Matthew stood fast in response to this extreme weather. Something peculiar was occurring. Something—

"The end is near!" someone shouted.

Matthew turned to his right and saw a man approaching him unintentionally through this abnormal gloom.

"The Kingdom of Heaven is in death!" the man cried frantically, as he was about to walk by Matthew.

"Wait!" Matthew grabbed the front of the man's wet tunic with both of his hands.

"Let me go!"

"What has happened?" Matthew demanded.

"Look." The man raised his right hand, then his left, toward the sky. "The Kingdom of God is in me!"

Matthew tightened his grasp on the shabby tunic and pulled the man closer to him. "Damn your eyes. Be clear about what you are saying."

"He! Has been crucified."

"Who has?"

"The Messiah!"

"Jesus?"

"Crucified! Yes! Crucified!"

Matthew shook the man. "Where? Where!"

"The Kingdom of Heaven—"

"Where!"

"From there! They say—he will come—he will come after—there—over there—"

"You! You are possessed!"

"Always coming." The man laughed hysterically. "Always coming."

Matthew tried to shake the demon out of him. "Where is he? Where!"

The madman grew alarmingly calm. "Golgotha."

Lightning struck close by.

Upon recognizing the name of this public place of execution, Matthew relaxed his grip on the man's tunic. "Golgotha."

The demon-possessed man broke free of Matthew's hold, leaned right into a single back step, and struck Matthew's left temple so hard with his fist that he dropped to his knees. The possessed man followed through with another stunning blow to that left temple, which made Matthew fall sideways to the ground.

The madman stooped over him, then cackled as he scratched the top of his head.

Matthew caught a momentary glimpse of him.

The possessed man shuffled away before he shouted, "Always present!"

Matthew could not move. And then, he could no longer see. But he could hear the man continue to shout in a frenzy.

"Always present—always occurring—always at death—at death: his Kingdom, his presence—you'll see—you'll see—"

77

A roll of thunder preceded a penetrating shriek by this demon-possessed man before Matthew lost all consciousness.

Chapter 12

Matthew rolled onto his back and groaned. Large raindrops pelted his face.

As he wrestled to understand his present condition, he blinked rapidly in response to the assaulting rainfall. He turned his head aside and rubbed his wet eyelids before he sat up.

He touched his injured temple and winced, then stood up not knowing how long he had been unconscious.

Distant thunder could be heard from somewhere within the disturbing darkness.

Matthew turned to his left and flinched after stepping on a sharp rock. He looked down and discovered bare feet.

The demon-possessed man—no, someone else must have stolen his leather sandals.

Behind a shudder and a sigh, he pretended to stand like a man who was surveying the terrain to orient himself toward Golgotha's direction and, therefore, he was pretending to appear fearless before God like a man. But he abandoned this performance knowing that God could not be fooled by this fraudulent stance.

After releasing a faint cry, he offered God a weak prayer.

"Lord, please give me the strength to be what I have pretended to be right now."

He knew his prayer was not going to be answered because he knew that his prayer was not being heard. He knew it. This was his punishment. This was—wait, *this* black sky. Was *this* a punishment as well?

He rubbed his eyelids, then scrutinized his surroundings. He could not comprehend this peculiar gloom. It was as if the sun had been covered by a thick curtain in order to provide the backdrop for the strange celestial occurrences above that he had never seen before.

Dangerous lightning struck close by and roused him out of his mystified condition and reminded him of his necessary destination.

"Golgotha. I must see my Lord."

The calm periods of time between the strikes of lightning were inhabited by the firmament's insistent flickers of crude light, which ordained the cruel way ahead.

When Matthew reached the edge of the city, he traveled northerly using Jerusalem's eastern wall as his guide within this haunting darkness and through this cruel weather. He doggedly crept along the city's perimeter to reach the western side of the wall, then he headed southerly along the wall toward Golgotha.

Rolls of continuous thunder followed by the frequent strikes of lightning in the distance, conspired with the intensifying rain and the increasing wind.

He leaned into the extreme slant of the rain and the savage gusts of wind, and struggled toward his destination knowing that the city's wall would guide him through this chaos and lead him to his Lord—at that place of execution called Golgotha.

Chapter 13

The peculiar weather conditions abated with the return of daylight long before Matthew reached the foothills of Golgotha.

Matthew could not continue up the hill, however, once he saw three crosses, once he actually witnessed the consummation of his Lord's execution.

The middle cross was empty, the other two crosses were occupied by ravaged men.

There were two Roman Legionnaire guards posted near the crosses to maintain general order on the mound.

"Where is my Lord?" he wondered aloud.

His bare feet hurt.

When he reached for his upper mantle to cover his head, he was reminded that this garment had been stolen as well. "Damn."

"He died and was taken down not long ago," a nearby woman said to him.

When he turned to her, he was surprised by her dry and immaculate condition. The hem of her full length tunic was not caked with mud. And the lower half of her face was veiled by a white linen upper mantle. Her brow was smooth and unblemished. Her calm and empathetic eyes supported her clear and refined voice. She was beautiful.

"It was written," she added. "All is written."

Matthew spread out his arms, then dropped them to his side. "Then why do I live? Why was I considered worthy? What am I to think?"

"Don't think. You were not worthy. God has forgiven your transgressions because our Lord has died for your sins." Her eyes grew solemn. "So you can live."

"Where does that come from?"

The veiled immaculate woman ignored his challenge. "We are forgiven."

"How do you know this?"

Once again, she chose to ignore him. "He said he was sacrificing himself for us to take away our sins."

"Is that truly possible?" Matthew asked.

"Are you questioning him again?"

"I won't deny that I have had my doubts."

"Many times."

"But he gave me many times to doubt him." He threw a defensive glance at her. "I have remained on my heels for three years."

"And you continue to remain so today."

Matthew rubbed his left temple in an attempt to reduce the pain of his headache. "I don't want today to continue. I want it to be yesterday. God help me."

"God has provided you with this help through his grace, and through your faith in our Lord, Jesus."

"I have failed to receive this help. And I have failed to understand this grace," said Matthew. "Look at me. I've been in hiding, in fear, and in guilt—for my lack of true faith."

"Have faith."

"I am not feeling it," he said.

"God is present."

In despair, Matthew indicated the empty cross. "Did you hear our Lord say anything before he died?"

"*My God, my God, why did you abandon me?*"

Matthew took several steps to complete a tight circle, and to demonstrate his astonishment. "You mean, my Lord believed that he was abandoned?"

"No. He felt that—" She paused and considered the remainder of her forthcoming answer before she said, "—that the terrifying weight of God's wrath, which he had to suffer while dying on that cross for us, was taking too long for him."

"Abandon me means *abandon me*—"

"Listen! Abandoned me meant *release me*," she explained. "*Listen*. Please. Jesus suffered the wrath of God while dying on the cross for your sins, and the sins of the world."

Matthew's eyes blinked rapidly as he thought about what she said to him. "Do you understand what it is that *you* are saying to me?"

"Do *you* understand what it is that *I am* saying to you?" The veiled immaculate woman took a single step toward him. "This was not a cry about abandonment. This was a cry about wanting to be released from further physical despair."

"And you heard that in the tone of his voice?"

"I did."

"But it *was* a cry—"

"About when his suffering was going to come to an end," she stated once again. "Like the cry of a woman longing for the end of her labor."

"Our Lord did not die like a woman failing in her struggle to give birth." He stepped back from her. "Having been abandoned, as you've said, is what—"

"He implied—when he asked why God, *His Father*, continued to let him suffer *His wrath* for so long."

Matthew's vexation deepened. "And you *witnessed* this."

"'*I am thirsty*,'" she continued. "'*It is finished*,' he cried victoriously. Then he shouted, '*Father, into your hands I place my spirit*!'" She leveled a steady gaze at him. "As if he voluntarily gave up his life."

"But he was arrested and executed, and the weight of suffering was pressing him toward death, woman."

"It was *witnessed*. And it is a mystery that cannot be *fully* understood."

"I don't understand *any* of this."

"Then listen: you can hear it, you can feel it, but you cannot see the wind itself."

Matthew did not know how to respond to her.

"Not witnessing this for yourself," she continued, "does not matter. Listen. He spoke of his death to you. Why can't you remember that?"

He clenched his teeth in response, then felt ashamed. "Who are you?"

"That I cannot tell you."

"But you must—"

Suddenly, he was frightened by a series of horrible shrieks from somewhere behind him. He turned toward the uproar and discovered fear-and-trembling embodied in a possessed woman.

The Legionnaire sentries were unaffected by the minor disorder caused by this deranged woman.

When the possessed woman caught sight of Matthew, she shouted, "He died!" Then she approached him and said, "He's dead!"

Matthew backed away from her. He was wary of having another encounter with a possessed person.

She wore a coarse sackcloth tunic, which manifested poverty rather than mourning. Her long upper mantle hung from her shoulders and touched the hard ground. Her unkempt black hair was not braided and came down upon her back in a tangled mess of strings. Her eyes were wild and her skin was diseased. Her large features were distorted by her madness.

The woman howled. "Jesus is dead!"

When Matthew realized that she was no longer addressing him, he turned to the veiled immaculate woman, who seemed to have wisdom.

She was no longer standing near him. And to his surprise, this beautiful woman was no longer standing anywhere.

He searched the vicinity for her, but she was nowhere to be seen. She had disappeared like a phantom.

"Where did she go?" He turned to the demon-possessed woman. "Where is—"

"The end of the world!" The demented woman shouted at the sky. "My God, my God, this was no man! He was the Messiah!" She sat down where she stood, exhausted by her rants, and released a long sigh, which led to a vacant stare at the crosses on the hill.

Matthew stepped away from her as he wrestled with a torrent of thoughts.

Not worthy to be near this demented woman; not worthy to have been addressed by that veiled immaculate woman; not worthy to be included among all these sorrowful women, who were standing before the Lord's empty cross.

Because of the weight of all this unworthiness, he was compelled to lower his right knee upon the hard and rocky ground.

From somewhere a woman announced, "He was the Son of God."

He lowered his left knee beside his bent right and bowed his head feeling too wretched to be included among these women. "These women."

Matthew covered his face with the palms of his hands and endeavored to understand what that immaculate woman, that veiled presence, that beautiful phantom had said about the reason for the Son of God's death.

PART III

SIMON THE PATRIOT

Chapter 14

"*I tell you the truth: one of you is going to betray me.*"

Jesus' unexpected declaration provoked a chorus of whispered resentment's, which heightened into a lively string of denials among the men seated at the supper table.

Simon slipped his right hand inside an opening in his tunic, grabbed the handle of a dagger, and waited for someone to accuse him of being the betrayer.

The influence of his past affiliation with zealous patriots, who resisted Rome with violence, had remained strong within him. Even after spending years protecting Jesus, he could not shake his intense hatred for Rome. He could not give up his dagger even though he had listened to his Lord speak about love, as well as speak about the loving of his enemy—an idea he could not understand.

He did not comprehend what was happening at the table.

Simon's eyes darted from side to side in an effort to avoid making eye contact with his Lord Jesus, but he failed. His eyes flattened with shame when he was caught by Jesus' disapproving gaze. He released the handle of his hidden dagger, knitted the fingers of his hands together, and placed the tense double-fist on the table. "Damn."

His disappointment concerning this personal failure deepened toward disgust, then anger—he had not succeeded in abandoning his violent inclinations. He was the same man who stood on the shore of Galilee on the day he was called by Jesus to come with him.

Simon's anger strengthened as his conflicting thoughts swirled within him and befuddled whatever good sense he had left inside of—

"It will be one of you twelve," said Jesus. *"One who dips his bread in the dish with me. The Son of man will die as the scriptures say he will; but how terrible for that man who will betray the Son of Man! It would have been better for that man if he had never been born!"*

Simon was terribly disturbed by what Jesus had said and joined the others in their unruly response at the table.

Because of his fierce instinctive nature toward self defense and self preservation, accompanied by intense pride, Simon rejected what he had heard. He sensed that his fellow disciples were feeling spiritually punished as well.

Simon felt vanquished.

He brooded alongside these men; he also brooded alongside this unknown man—the would-be betrayer.

His brown beard was full, his mustache was thick, and his hair was combed straight back. His head was partially covered with a loosely draped upper mantle, which also partially covered his mouth.

This unconscious habit of concealing his identity persisted even now, at his Lord's table, because of his long association with warlike patriots against Rome. He had black eyes, long ears, a hawk-like nose, and full lips. He was a tall and powerfully built man with large and strong hands.

Simon possessed a formidable presence.

His calf length tunic, made of inferior wool, was cinched around his waist with a leather belt. His crude sandals, made of hard leather, were secured to his feet by thin straps that were wrapped around his ankles.

Simon was always ready to resist his occupier, always ready to revolt against his oppressor. As far as he was concerned, Rome had no place in Judea and Galilee and Samaria—all, the land of his people—all, the land occupied by Rome.

He respected bravery and appreciated the courage that his Lord possessed. But to Simon's persistent bewilderment, Jesus disapproved of any zealous tendency for physical violence against an aggressor.

Simon loved serving the Lord with a dogged passion, and strove to measure up to Jesus' ardency for love—*love* of all things, without bloodshed or hatred or deceit.

To Simon's dismay, his Lord's insistence about replacing violence with love was not of this world, but of a world that his Lord referred to as the Kingdom of Heaven.

He often did not understand what his Lord said, but he knew he wanted to serve and protect him from the crowds that sometimes turned into threatening mobs.

Simon was fully aware, however, that it was through his Lord's divine grace that he managed to control some of his recklessness and most of his rebellious inclinations; and it was through his Lord's divine grace that he became acceptable to the Lord and, therefore, useful in *His* service.

Jesus brought order and silence at the table—then waited.

Judas stood up, approached Jesus, and accepted his Lord's offer of bread. Judas dipped the bread into a dish of sauce and ate it. Then he drank all the wine that was in the cup that Jesus gave him before he left the room.

What they were offered next was contrary to standard religious observances.

The body?

Simon paused, then ate it.

The blood?

Simon hesitated, then drank it.

It was simple bread from Jesus' hand and plain wine from Jesus' cup—right?

Simon surveyed the table to see if any of his brethren had understood what their Lord Jesus had delivered to them.

Everyone seemed to be as perplexed as he was—and as nervously possessed by this new wonder.

While this body and this blood continued to baffle Simon, Peter became angry and resentful after Jesus said, "*This very night all of you will run away and leave me.*"

Simon, along with the others, was truly upset about this. But Peter made it so personal that he stood up and pounded the table with his fists, then turned to Jesus and said, "I will never leave you even if all the rest do!"

"*I tell you this Peter,*" Jesus answered, "*the cock will not crow today until you have said three times that you do not know me.*"

Simon understood Peter's anger, but he was also grateful that Jesus had not condemned him with that terrible prediction. He was so grateful, in fact, that he openly supported Peter's continued resentment.

"I will never say I do not know you," Peter insisted, "even if I have to die with you."

With an insincere enthusiasm born of self-interest, each man supported Peter's indignation by pounding on the table in rebellion as well.

Amid this revolt, Simon struggled to comprehend the meaning of eating *His* body, and drinking *His* blood.

Jesus gave him bread. Jesus gave him wine. Didn't he?

Chapter 15

Simon continued to be plagued by his contentious thoughts while he and his brethren accompanied Jesus on the journey across the Kidron Valley to reach their destination—The Garden of Gethsemane.

His lack of understanding about what happened during their last supper harassed him to such an extent that he needed to justify—no—he needed to recollect that life changing moment when he was approached by his Lord for the first time.

At that moment, Simon thought that he had been discovered by a revolutionary Messiah—a warrior of resistance against Rome. Instead, he had been discovered by a spiritual Messiah—a shepherd of souls submitting to Rome, who needed to be protected from aggressive crowds by an ordinary man, by a brute fisherman, by a mere disciple.

Simon rubbed his eyelids with his fingertips.

Jesus was certainly revolutionary, but in his *own* way.

Simon stepped harder upon the ground.

Jesus should have been the one to overthrow Rome.

Simon smashed his right fist into the palm of his left hand.

Jesus never planned to take up arms against Rome.

Simon slapped his right side.

Jesus had blessed him with three remarkable years.

Simon nodded to himself, then inhaled great determination to continue following Jesus.

Somehow, the Lord had his complete allegiance. Somehow, there was a sincere union of hearts between him and his Lord. Somehow, he loved him and believed in him and trusted in Jesus because ... because—

Simon slapped his chest with his right hand.

Occasionally, he would catch a glimpse of his Lord Jesus' truth. Yes—occasionally, he saw that his openhearted Lord was a much greater Messiah than the promised one that was expected to come. And yes—occasionally, he saw that his Lord's Kingdom, which was not of this world, was also much greater than the promised one that was expected to come.

Simon shook his head in dismay.

None of these glimpses of faith lasted.

He did not know why he continued to struggle to affirm that his Lord was truly the Messiah, who had no use for bloodshed or hatred or deceit; and who spoke of love, of truth, of forgiveness—even to his enemies, the enemies of his ... his—

Simon's inner turmoil escaped, unintentionally, into a verbal self-incrimination.

"Lord, help me. I'm lying to myself. It seems as if I cannot be fully convinced. I have not lost my doubts, and I have not lost my recklessness to cause dissatisfaction among my brother disciples. I have not learn to ... to ...."

He checked himself and glanced at the others to see if they had heard him muttering this nonsense to himself as they entered the Garden of Gethsemane. But if they had, his Lord seized the moment and prevented any chaffing remarks that might have come from one of them when his Lord Jesus stopped walking, turned to them, and spoke.

"*Pray that you will not fall into temptation. Sit here while I go over there and pray.*"

Then Jesus left him and the others where they stood and continued further into the Garden after selecting three of his brethren to accompany him.

Knowing his Lord's habits, Simon predicted that they would be abandoned as well after his Lord chose a solitary place to pray.

Simon sat down, then reclined with the intent to sleep, despite his Lord's instructions to pray. He wanted to escape from his thoughts instead, which he did, until he was awakened by his Lord. When he stood up, he heard a series of excuses and apologies by the others and—

"*Enough!*" Jesus shouted. "*The hour has come! Look, the Son of Man is now handed over to the power of sinful men. Look, here is the man who is betraying me!*"

A large mob, armed with makeshift clubs and escorted by Temple Guards armed with long swords, invaded the Garden.

Simon gasped when Judas appeared. "My God! It's you—"

Judas kissed his Lord.

"—you traitor!"

Jesus was arrested.

There was anger on both sides.

Simon slipped his right hand inside of his tunic, grabbed the handle of his dagger, and pulled it out of its sheath.

There was a cry of pain.

Jesus chastised someone for cutting off a man's ear.

Men shouted in response.

Simon threatened a Temple Guard with his drawn dagger.

The mob's aggression intensified.

A man struck Thomas with a wooden mallet.

Simon was prepared to kill any man who tried to prevent him from escaping.

Men scattered in all directions.

Simon dodged the sidestroke from a wooden end of a hoe, then countered the attack by slicing the assailant's forearm before he ran and ran and ran.

Chapter 16

After Simon hid inside a thick growth of shrubs, he waited for a long time to see if he was being pursued. With his dagger held at the ready, he was determined to fight with anyone who attacked him.

"God help me."

He hated Rome more than he loved Jesus; he wanted independence more than he wanted his own salvation; he believed in the law more than having faith in his Lord; he was a militant revolutionary against Rome more than he was a disciple of Jesus; he believed in hard resistance more than soft tenderness; he believed in the power of terrorism against Roman dominion; he believed in . . . in nothing—yes—nothing, because he—Simon—was all talk and anger and full of confusion now that he was alone and without the constant reassurance of his . . . his Lord, Jesus.

"Jesus!"

He stood up.

"Where are you now?"

Simon squatted inside the dense shrubs again and waited to see if anybody heard his defiant cry.

"Where am I?"

He did not want to kill anybody.

"God help me."

Simon glanced at the dagger that he held in his right hand.

"Sick."

He was repulsed suddenly by his behavior.

"You are sick."

He had sworn to use it if . . . if—

"God forgive me. Lord, save me."

He stabbed the ground with the dagger, wanting the world to die—and left it there.

"Who are you now?"

Simon turned away from that dagger.

He wanted that savage expression of despair to be his final attack against the world. But he realized that there was no escape from himself. Because he decided—

"Nothing is final."

Chapter 17

At daybreak, Simon sat up then rose to his feet. He searched the surrounding area, then stepped out of the tall brush.

He decided to go to Jerusalem.

The walk across the Kidron Valley took longer than it did the day before because he stopped often to assess the countryside. After having to escape that mob yesterday, he sensed danger everywhere. His caution remained steadfast as he drew closer to his destination. But his caution intensified, suddenly, when a peculiar darkness blotted out the daylight with a gloom that seemed like the end of the world.

"Bah! Let it come."

He spat on the ground.

"Let it come."

Lightning struck the earth. Distant rolls of thunder could be heard. Odd celestial activities above could be seen.

"Mere lightning and thunder."

He scrutinized that unfamiliar sky.

"But those signs above. Those are—wait."

Simon stopped walking.

"Bah. Bad weather. That's all this is."

Jesus would have put an end to this like he ended that storm on the lake. The wind and the sea obeyed him in Galilee. And the weather here would have also obeyed his commands.

Simon exhaled emptiness.

"But where are you now, Lord? And where are the others?"

He scratched his head during a genuine effort to think clearly.

"I'm sure I saw Matthew run into a tall tree trunk. And the others—well, the others, were also afraid of that mob."

Simon massaged his eyelids.

"Damn. I acted like a fool—and a coward. I should have stood my ground."

He struck his chest with his right fist.

"Quit thinking you fool!"

A strong wind slanted the abrupt start of a heavy rain.

Simon walked into that slanted rainstorm with his head down and pushed through it without stopping until he came close one of Jerusalem's gate. He paused, momentarily, to be sure that there were no Temple Guards or Roman Legionnaires posted nearby before he approached the gate.

He was challenged by a gatekeeper. "Who goes there?"

"Nobody." Simon approached the frightened man. "What sort of dark weather is this? Do you know?"

"Who could know what this is?" the gatekeeper answered.

"Why isn't your main gate open?"

"I was ordered to keep it closed this morning."

"But why?"

"I don't question orders."

"I need to pass through."

"The needle's eye is unlocked." A roll of thunder distracted the gatekeeper. "Someone told me that this ominous weather came with the death of that famous prophet."

"What prophet?"

"The one called Jesus."

"He's dead?"

"Crucified with two other men."

"Crucified." Simon pressed the palm of his right hand against his forehead.

"You act as if you know him."

Simon was unable to suppress his anguish. "He . . . he is my Lord."

Strange laughter preceded the gatekeeper's calloused response. "Then you, my friend, are without a Lord."

"Crucified." Simon lowered his right hand to his side. "Where?"

"On Golgotha—the place of the skull."

"Golgotha," Simon muttered. "Tell me, please, in what direction do you believe is the quickest way there?"

"The shortest way is through the city. But right now, it's not the quickest way. The gatekeeper pointed to his left. "Along the city wall going that way is certainly not the shortest route. But for now, I believe it is the easiest and the safest way to get there."

"Easiest?" Simon leveled a suspicious gaze at the gate-keeper. "And safest?"

"You will come to see this for yourself. Trust me." He pointed to the left once more. "Golgotha cannot be missed."

Chapter 18

Simon's journey toward Golgotha took much longer than he expected.

As he traveled along the eastern and western walls, Simon had to dodge several squads of Auxiliary Legionnaires and, occasionally, hide from small detachments of hard riding Roman Calvary. But he perceived that Rome's presence near the city's wall was inconsistent, and the Legionnaires seemed to lack fervor.

Simon was more afraid, however, of the roving groups of aggressive bandits, who where truly dangerous, and who were taking advantage of Rome's somewhat temperate conduct during this unnatural gloom. Dodging these savages was a serious matter of survival.

Ragged scavengers searched for vulnerable pilgrims, who were traveling on foot or riding on asses, and who were easy prey for assault and robbery.

Well armed highwayman waited for the merchant caravans and the escorted rich, who were traveling by camel or cart and who were worthy of being attacked and pillaged.

In all cases, pilgrims that continued to travel to reach Jerusalem under these conditions were being careless.

Roving bandits, vicious scavengers, organized marauders—all, waited for those who had not taken precautions against an attack during this sinister and disagreeable weather.

Normal darkness often provided fertile ground for lawlessness. This abnormal cloak of darkness, however, encouraged anarchy to bloom across the countryside.

"Easier going this way—it might be, mister gatekeeper, but . . . ."

Simon grunted.

"But if this is the safest way to reach Golgotha, I wonder how much worse it is in Jerusalem at this hour?"

Foolishly, Simon continued to ponder about the general surrounding conditions rather than remaining vigilant concerning his own safety.

Violence presented itself without mercy, suddenly, through an assault from behind by a blow to his right shoulder near the neck.

Simon fell to his knees, shook himself in an effort to recover from the blow, and tried to stand up.

"I've got him!"

As soon as Simon turned his head to see who attacked him, the bandit struck the left side of his face.

Simon fell onto his right side and rolled face down on the ground.

"He doesn't look like he has anything. But he does looks dangerous," said the leading bandit, who rolled Simon onto his back with his foot. "Look at this."

"Be careful," his comrade said. "He's still conscious."

"Yes, I see. And he's a tough one, I think."

His comrade knelt beside Simon and searched him, while a third bandit took charge of being a lookout.

"Ah. This one has a sheath."

"Where's the dagger?" their leader asked.

The comrade who was searching Simon grabbed him by the front of his tunic and pulled him off the ground. "You heard him. Where is it?"

"Lost," said Simon.

The bandit released the tunic as he shoved Simon back onto the ground. "He's no good to us. A sheath. That's all he has."

"Take it, anyway."

"And leave him," said the lookout. "We need to move on."

The comrade who carried out the search stood up, then kicked Simon's left side. "You're worthless."

"Kill him," said the lead bandit.

"Legionnaire cavalry!" the lookout warned.

The bandits turned toward the approaching danger.

"They're riding hard."

"Let's go."

"That way," the bandit leader said. "Come on."

The bandits dashed away leaving Simon alive.

Simon waited for the cavalry to pass by before he sat up. He took a deep breath as he massaged his aching neck.

"Damn their eyes. Damn them."

He stood up with great difficulty, but with a greater determination to continue his journey to Golgotha.

His first steps were so unsteady that he had to stop and plant himself where he stood until he was confident about his balance.

He massaged his aching left side, cursed his heartless assailants, then proceeded toward his destination.

By the time Simon arrived at Golgotha, the menacing weather had abated and the sun had brought gray light to this sorrowful place. Golgotha was hopelessly windswept; the end of the world seemed near.

Numerous groups of women occupied the mound, and occupied the surrounding foothills that comprised its outer rim. Their eyes seemed weather beaten, their clothes seemed storm damaged. Their firm bearing, however, seemed to be defiant—and courageous.

Simon was wary of the two Auxiliary Legionnaire sentries as he approached the crosses, which were set upon the highest point on the mount. Fortunately, the sentries seemed bored and disinterested in him.

When he managed to clear his mind enough to cast his undivided attention upon the center cross, Simon had to acknowledge a harsh and disappointing reality: he had missed the opportunity to be present during his Lord's death for all time.

He knelt before the empty cross and touched the rough hewed wood that had been his Lord's instrument of suffering and death. He couldn't, he wouldn't, cry.

Simon pulled his right hand away from the cross and touched his right cheek. This was as close to being a witness to his Lord's crucifixion as he was ever going to be.

He stood up, backed away from the empty cross, and shifted his attention to the occupied cross on his right in response to a groan from a hard man like himself. Then he shifted his gaze to the soft and silent young man on his left, who was also stripped naked—like his Lord must have been.

The young man appeared to be dead. And to Simon's surprise, a peaceful expression adorned his face.

The older man to his right growled at him, then closed his savage eyes—the cruel torture that he was enduring marked his face with suffering. His upper arms were lashed to the cross beam, but his wrists were nailed to that wood. His ankles were nailed to the lower side of the vertical beam that served as a stake, which was impaled into the hard ground. His naked body was forced to straddle a shameful support beam, which must have caused extreme pain to the exposed private region between his legs—adding more suffering to a lingering and agonizing death. The older man's crossbeam, like the younger man's, was set higher on the vertical stake than on the empty cross between them.

Simon shifted his gaze back to the center cross to verify this observation.

The Lord's crossbeam had been set lower on the stake. And near the top of the vertical beam there was a placard nailed into the heart of the wood just above where Jesus would have pressed the back of his head. Upon the placard there was an inscription.

Despite his limited ability to read, Simon managed to make out the words that were written upon it: *Jesus of Nazareth, the King of the Jews.*

Simon pressed the palm of his right hand against his chest to steady himself.

He rejected fear. He would not tremble here.

"It is alright to be afraid," someone said.

Simon peered at a veiled elderly woman. "Who are you?"

"Nobody."

"That's just what I need. A strange nobody." He lowered his right hand to his side.

"Don't get hard against me, young man."

White hair peeked out from underneath her upper mantle, which veiled the lower half of her face. Her brow was wrinkled and, from the corners of her eyes, crows feet crept toward her temples. Her light-brown eyes, however, sparkled like a young woman. It was apparent, by her thin tunic, that she possessed a skeletal body.

Simon shifted his gaze back to his Lord's cross.

"I am also love and joy and peace," she added.

"What did you say?" He gave his full attention to her and discovered that this persistent woman was very short.

"I am patience, kindness, and goodness."

He sneered. "Who are you?"

"I am faithfulness, gentleness, and self-control."

He studied the surrounding area and discovered, to his astonishment, that nobody seemed interested in his encounter with this tenacious woman.

"Our Lord forgave sins," she continued.

"How did he do that?"

"Look." The veiled elderly woman pointed at the empty cross with her fragile right hand. "He is our Lord."

"I think I have lost my faith in that." He grunted. Then he leveled a hard gaze at her. "What is the matter with me?"

"You're thinking too hard."

"I already know that." He slapped his thigh with his left hand to express his self-contempt. "Why can't I understand this forgiveness of sins?"

"You had three years to ask *him*."

Simon was startled by her remark, then responded to her defensively. "You know how Jesus was."

"Since you were with *him* for three years, explain that to me."

"Impossible."

"Explain *that*."

He altered his flustered expression by wiping the left corner of his mouth with the back of his right hand. "He was commanding. His words penetrated into, into—my being, my thoughts as he continued to be . . . be—"

"Kind?"

"To me. Yes." He grinned. "And to everyone."

"Who saw. And who understood."

"Who understood." He snorted. "To everyone no matter who it was—yes. Even to a sinful woman who wet his feet with her tears, then dried them with her hair."

"Did that seem strange to you at the time? Don't lie to me."

113

Simon hesitated. "I admit, I felt uneasy."

"And you were embarrassed when she kissed his feet, and then poured perfume upon them."

"Yes! Yes. And *all* in my presence. Imagine that."

The veiled elderly woman folded her hands together. "Our Lord was always very free about—"

"Free!"

One of the sentries took notice of him.

Simon waited in silence until the sentry lost interest in him.

"Free is an understatement," he said.

"And he forgave her, her sins."

"He often forgave sins. Yes."

"And he always explained why."

"Yes. And . . . and I was always convinced each time. But afterwords . . . ."

She encouraged him to continue. "But afterwords . . . ."

"I could not remember his answers."

"Why?"

"Because I'm a dumb fisherman who can barely read and write. Who barely understood what our Lord meant or did when he forgave or . . . or whatever—I can't remember. Bah!" He turned away from the veiled elderly woman. "Let's get back to something I *do* remember." He cleared his throat. "After wiping my Lord's feet with her hair, she kissed his feet and . . . and—"

"Poured perfume upon them and—"

"Sexual. That was all very sexual. And in my presence, *and* in the presence of my brethren as well. Shameful."

"Our Lord knew what he was doing," she reminded him.

"And what was he doing?"

"You should have asked him then, if it bothered you so deeply."

"I was distracted by what I saw."

"That's a lie!" she charged.

Simon was startled by her sudden forcefulness. "I'm simply saying . . . ."

"What?"

"Nothing. Nothing." He shrugged. "I loved him." Then he looked into her bright, but stern, eyes. "Damn it. I *do* believe in him."

"Then you are saved."

"Sure, sure," was his cynical answer. "If you say so."

"Our Lord said so."

"But my sins, my sins—"

"Have been forgiven," she insisted. "Look at his cross again. It has been the place of ultimate sacrifice, of ultimate suffering."

He studied the empty cross. "Ultimate. Sacrifice. Ultimate. Suffering." He dropped to his knees and closed his eyes to hide, like a child, from his shame. "For him. I know. For him."

"But a*ll* for you. *All* for those who are chosen to understand. And for *all* who have remained standing upon their belief on Golgotha."

The silence that followed grew heavy and long enough for Simon to recover from his self-reproach.

"Who are you? Please." But when he turned his head toward the veiled elderly woman, she had vanished.

He stood up and stumbled in one direction, then into another, in search of her. In disarray, Simon continued to search in all directions—close by, and afar. She was nowhere to be seen on Golgotha.

Simon behaved like man who was demon-possessed.

PART IV

THOMAS THE DOUBTER

Chapter 19

Thomas blinked into the morning light when he opened his eyes, then covered them with his left hand. He neither wanted to face his present uncertainty, nor wanted to accept his past disgrace of running away—he did not stay with Jesus to protect him from that mob.

He uncovered his eyes and sat up to face the day—he licked his dry lips.

His head was sore. He raised his hand to explore his right temple, discovered a lump, and winced when he pressed it with his fingertips.

"You broke the scab, you idiot."

He stared at his bloodstained fingertips, as he rubbed them with his thumb, and vaguely remembered something about his Lord's body—and blood.

"The injury to your head is a coward's wound."

Thomas wiped his fingers against the side of his tunic, which left a blood smear of dishonor.

"Damn you for being a coward."

He leaned forward in an attempt to ease his distress. When that failed, he rose to his feet and managed to remain standing.

"Where are you now?"

Thomas tried to assess where he was on the Mount of Olives. He could not remember how long and how far he ran before he was assaulted a second time by several members of that roving mob. The right side of his head ached. His eyes burned.

He shook himself in an attempt to clear his mind.

"Damn this misery."

He scratched his jaw, then stumbled into an uneven walk not knowing where he was going.

Thomas was a big boned muscular man with the scarred, and once calloused, hands of a fisherman. He wore a full length tunic with half sleeves that came down to the top of his hairy forearms. The tunic was made of coarsely woven wool, and it was tied at the waist with a rope that was made fancy with a series of nautically woven knots. His sandals and feet were mud stained.

He stopped walking, touched the side of his throbbing head, and winced again. He cursed his sticky fingertips, then marked the front of his tunic to display the sanguine of disgrace.

Thomas's short and disheveled hair was partially covered by an upper mantle, which had been placed carelessly upon his head. His dark eyes were deeply inset and his ears were pinned back. His nose and mouth were too small for his broad face. His thick black beard covered a large and unbreakable jaw.

An attack of dizziness forced him to stop walking. He looked up at the sky in an effort to steady himself and, to his dismay, the gray daylight unexpectedly faded into an unnatural darkness. Thomas sat on the ground to prevent himself from falling as a heavy rain began to fall.

A vicious wind accompanied so many slashes of lightning, that the simultaneous streaks appeared to permanently disfigure the sky.

He closed his eyes and collapsed onto his right side as he listened to the numerous claps of thunder roll across the Kidron Valley from Jerusalem's direction.

Thomas inhaled deeply and lost consciousness on his exhale, then drifted into an unusual dream that was heard but not seen, except for a brief moment when he caught a glimpse of the man who spoke to him. The visual moment was long enough to permit Thomas to identify the man by his trade—a potter, who possessed the characteristic clay stains on his tunic and who had dry brown clay imbedded in his fingernails. The potter, however, had the lower half of his face veiled with an unstained upper mantle.

"The Kingdom of God is within you," said the veiled potter.

"How can I understand that?" Thomas implored. "Where is this *within you*? I have searched."

"Jesus said that whoever tries to save his own life will lose it."

"Didn't Jesus also say that the Kingdom did not come in such a way as to be seen?"

"He wasn't speaking to you," said the veiled potter.

"I was standing there when he was—"

"Speaking through you. To the others. The nonbe-
lievers. To the Pharisees who challenged him with under-
handed questions."

Thomas grinned. "Yes. They were always trying to
trick him."

"They tricked themselves."

"Tell me then, sincerely, that I haven't been tricked.
Have I been tricked? Don't be angry with me."

"I will not be angry with you. I understand the source
of your doubt."

Thomas was astounded. "You do?"

"In your darkness, you have searched for belief over
here, then searched over there, and searched here and
searched there until, here you are—"

"Lost."

"In this dark place of nowhere—feeling unborn."

"It is a feeling of emptiness," said Thomas.

"Nobody knows from where the wind arises or where
it goes or when it will come—and so it is with anyone
who is born again."

"Is that the Kingdom of God *within you*?"

The veiled potter considered the question. "You keep
hoping for that lightning to strike and illuminate you—
like a trick."

Thomas was embarrassed. "You speak my mind."

"But your hope has brought you here, in this dark
place of nowhere—the nowhere, without the Lord."

"My Lord didn't save himself during his arrest."

"He *couldn't*," said the veiled potter.

"Then I continue to be lost."

"Because he also *wouldn't*."

"What am I to think of that?"

"His arrest was written. He told you that."

Thomas slapped his chest. "Why can't I remember that? Why?"

"Because you keep trying to save yourself."

"There's nothing wrong with that!" Thomas rasped.

"It can't be done, I said! The Lord told you many times that in trying to save yourself, you will lose yourself."

"It's simply natural to want to—I can't help it."

"That's why I am here."

Thomas grew suspicious. "Why?"

"To inform you that it has been done—by our Lord, Jesus."

"It has been done?" Thomas scoffed. "There's no comfort in this for me. Done? What has been done?"

"The ultimate sacrifice for your sins."

Thomas hesitated. "Yes. True. I remember that . . . that he foretold this sacrifice to me—to all of my brethren."

"Then *believe* in him."

"In a world that has lost its way?"

"It is always so."

Thomas grunted. "God help me."

"Jesus has."

Thomas sighed long and hard and toward a semiconscious condition.

He rolled onto his back and felt daylight assaulting his closed eyelids as he struggled toward full consciousness.

Chapter 20

Thomas opened his eyes and blinked at the open sky. He turned his head and discovered that someone was sitting beside him. He sat up.

To his dismay, it was the veiled potter from his dream. "Go away you. You're not real."

"Haven't I been?"

"Go away, I said. This is not a dream."

"I am here."

"Bah! Why? Look at me. If I had trusted in the Lord, I would not have run away." He snarled. "This lack of trust seems to have continued with your—with *you*, whoever *you* are."

"The Lord would be angry with you if he heard these doubts."

"He heard my doubts often." Thomas grumbled. "And I confess, he was often angry with me. But not as often as he was angry with the people in the countryside who pressed him for more. Always more." He rubbed his eyelids. "He was frequently angry."

"Saddened, you mean."

"Don't alter the facts!"

"He was the Lord."

"I know, I know!" Thomas ran the fingers of his left hand through his hair. "Then why do I continue to act like an unbelieving man?"

"You have been thinking beyond the Lord."

"I don't understand that." Thomas sat up in response to his growing annoyance. "And I said, *don't* change the facts as they are."

"What are the facts?"

"Alright. Alright." Thomas conceded. "I always wanted more from him."

"And less of his teaching."

"Hold on there."

"Often enough."

"I don't know anything anymore." Thomas groaned. "It's true. I always waited for him to do something more when he taught."

"Something more. I see."

"What does that mean?"

"Your attention was held by the anticipation of more proof—say it. This *something more* was your desire to witness another miracle. Say it."

"Alright, yes—miracles. I always wanted more proof!" A forceful exhale expressed Thomas's defeat. "I often wonder why he chose me to follow him. Of all the fishermen in Galilee, why me?"

"Now there's a miracle for you."

Thomas was surprised by his own snicker. "A miracle of miracles, I think." Then he grew solemn. "The truth is,

I'm simply no better than those among the crowds who pressured my Lord for another miracle."

"Why?"

"Because wanting more miracles proved my continued doubt. I'm not supposed to have doubt in . . . in—"

"The Lord. Say it. *Say it.*"

"*The Lord.* God help me."

"I believe you have it right, this time."

Thomas welcomed his approval. "*My* Lord."

"And so, miracles are why he was often angry with you."

"With us. Yes. Of course, of course. We were already within the presence of the miracle of miracles."

"To follow him. *Him.*"

"We were always walking with the Lord," said Thomas.

"Then how come you were not *always* satisfied, even after having witnessed all of our Lord's truthfulness?"

The ground beneath Thomas's being was no longer certain about anything. "Because, I suppose, *always* is—is also not enough?"

"Somewhere in that *always* of yours, there could be the truth."

"I don't understand that."

"God help you."

Thomas clenched his teeth. "What is truth?"

"Are you alright?"

"I don't know."

"That's a raw looking wound on your head."

Thomas pulled off his damp upper mantle and noticed that it was bloodstained. "It hurts." With care, he touched the wound and discovered that it had stopped bleeding. "When I first woke up, there was a morning light, then a strange darkness covered the sun and brought with it a hard storm."

"That's right."

"Now it's light again," said Thomas. "How long was I unconscious this last time?"

"That doesn't matter."

"Alright. Don't tell me." He gathered some strength while taking a deep breath. "But now I need to find out what has happened to my Lord—and to the others." With great effort, Thomas shifted his right leg underneath his left as he leaned against his straightened right arm, which he used as a brace to keep himself from falling onto his right side.

"Easy there." The veiled potter almost placed his right hand upon Thomas's left shoulder to prevent him from rising to his feet. "There is no need to hurry now."

Thomas was perplexed by that assertion. "Who are you? And why is there no need to hurry?"

"Because it has come to pass."

"What has? What are you saying?"

"The Son of Man—"

"Wait. My Lord?" Thomas's eyes widened. "The arrest. I know. The arrest! What has happened? Where is my Lord, Jesus?"

"Crucified."

Thomas struggled to his knees. "My Jesus? My God. I didn't believe him."

"Believe *in* him."

"Crucified, you say."

"Yes. And died."

"Died."

"And taken down from the cross."

"Taken down."

"The cross is empty. You are too late. You have been warned."

There was a tone of finality in the veiled potter's voice.

"I was not there with him. God help me. Please." Thomas slumped forward and remained on his hands and knees for a long time. "Where is this empty cross?"

"On Golgotha."

Grief left him breathless. "Golgotha."

The veiled potter pointed at a distant place. "Over there. Look. Golgotha."

Thomas sat back on his knees. "Where?"

"There. Over there. On the other side of Jerusalem. Outside its western wall."

Thomas turned his head toward the indicated location and studied the distance that separated him from what was now a terrible destination. "I wasn't there."

"Don't be sorry."

Thomas stood up. "But I ran."

"You ran."

When Thomas started walking toward Golgotha, the veiled potter accompanied him from behind.

"We promised we wouldn't run," said Thomas.

"There were a lot of promises at the supper table."

"Yes, yes. But I pounded the top of that table with the rest of them. And as I did so, I prayed for courage—for the courage not to run."

"That was not a prayer that you needed to make."

"But when I heard him say—"

"Nothing."

"But he said that it was—"

"Written."

Thomas stopped walking and addressed the man. "My Lord told me—"

"To *pray* so you wouldn't fall into temptation."

"I pray!" Thomas turned away from him. "I pray." He started walking again. "And I have fallen."

"Have faith." The veiled potter continued to follow him.

Thomas stepped up his pace. "*I have fallen.*"

"The Lord understands."

"I never wanted Jesus to know me as I am now."

"He already knew who you are now."

"Then my Lord must also know the sad quality of my faith."

"There you are. See? You have faith in Jesus."

Thomas hissed. "It seems you have more faith in me than I do."

"Trust in Jesus. And you will be right with God."

"How can that be when my feelings are no more developed than a child's."

"The Kingdom of God is close to that child. Didn't you hear Jesus say that?"

"There it is again—this Kingdom of God. The Kingdom of . . . ." Thomas increased his pace across the Kidron Valley as he attempted to untangle his thoughts. "It must be something like eternal life, and these children belonging to the Kingdom. And something about no one being good and no one can save himself. I don't know. It's all become a muddle." He slowed his pace suddenly in response to his debilitating jumble of thoughts. "I have left everything for my Lord. That much I do know."

"And so you have hope."

"And I must hold onto that hope even though I continue not to understand the many things he has said to me. Right?"

"The Lord will have mercy on you. You'll see. Your faith in him will make it so."

"Salvation for a lost sinner." Thomas struggled with this notion. "That's new."

"Through the Lord—that's redemption."

"Redemption. Salvation. Redemption."

"Deliverance. Atonement. Deliverance," the veiled potter added, as he came alongside Thomas.

Thomas waived his hands at him. "Alright, alright! If I am to understand—no, believe in what you say, *you* must unveil yourself."

"This veil represents the partition from what has happened to what is coming."

"I neither understand nor trust that answer!"

"Then trust in the Lord."

"Uncover yourself, I said."

"You see?" The veiled potter maneuvered behind Thomas again. "You are anchored in time, but not in eternity."

"And I fear I will be anchored in this time before my Lord's empty cross."

"No! It is from that cross that he has passed through the veil and has entered into eternity—taking you with him."

"Into what eternity is that?" Thomas demanded.

"Into eternal life, if you will follow him—if you will believe in him."

"Damn you. This veil of yours has me standing between two worlds. How do I follow? How do I believe in—"

"*Him. In Him*—into the life beyond, into eternal life, into the Kingdom of God."

Thomas stopped walking. "The Kingdom of God. But I *do* believe in—wait. Who *are* you?" He turned around and discovered that the veiled potter was no longer behind him—or anywhere. He had vanished. "What? Where are you? *What* are you?"

He spat on the ground, then proceeded toward Golgotha.

Chapter 21

Thomas was too late.

He had been warned.

To see this reality, to experience this truth, and to be on the actual ground of being was another matter.

Thomas stood among the women and pondered the empty cross that must have been his Lord's instrument of execution.

The mound was populated by numerous women. Their fragile chorus of weeping reflected Thomas's utter despair in this place of death called Golgotha.

Despite his fear of the two Roman sentries who were posted nearby, he knelt within the shadow of the empty cross.

The Legionnaire, who stood guard near one of the crosses, appeared to be bored. He was a tall and rugged man. His broad chest, back, and shoulders were protected by a body armor comprised of articulated plates, and his head and neck were protected by a leather helmet. A sheathed short-sword was attached to a leather halter strap that hung from his neck. With his left hand, he held a large curved shield that was made of wood and was covered by leather. And with his right hand, he held a seven-foot pilum upright.

The other Legionnaire, who sat listlessly upon a flat stone, was half asleep. He was short and stocky and somewhat disassembled: his shield and pilum were on the ground beside him, his helmet was on his lap.

The women on the mound were not fooled by the disinterested demeanor exhibited by these mercenary guards. They knew that underneath those resigned expressions were fierce men, who were always ready to initiate Rome's brutality.

Thomas was comforted by the sincere feminine weeping that surrounded him.

He beheld the two men, who had been crucified with his Lord.

They were real men.

Thomas felt like a cur compared to them.

Criminals. Both. But men.

Thomas felt less than both of them.

Crucified. All three. According to Rome's definition of justice.

"Damn, Rome."

He peered at the young dead man and experienced a peculiar envy. Then he gazed at the hard, older man, who growled at his suffering, and who was probably guilty of past crimes that he had managed to carry out without being apprehended.

"Damn. Yes. You are superior to me. I *am* a dog."

Thomas turned away from that man's suffering and sought comfort by gazing at his Lord's cross. A dark stain of blood on the ground at the foot of that cross caught his attention.

Drops of his Lord's blood must have fallen from—from *His* wound.

Thomas stood up and approached that sacred ground.

To his surprise, the stained ground near the vertical stake of his Lord's cross was soft enough for him to scoop up some of it with his hands and bring that hallowed ground close to his face.

"Murderers. Animals."

His anger was mixed with despair.

Neither Legionnaire stirred.

Thomas pressed this blood-stained earth against his chest.

When he released the pressure against that earth and tilted open the palms of his hands, that hallowed ground turned into a dry dust, which dissipated across the mound by a single, but definite, gust of wind. Because of the depth of his despondency, Thomas was neither startled nor bewildered by this wind's transformational influence.

Several women walked by the sentries, who took no notice of them, and stepped between Thomas and the Lord's cross as if he was not there. Because after all, to them, Thomas was just another man—just another man.

Thomas turned away from them and the crosses, walked down the hill, and approached the outer rim of the mound where he belonged—among the lesser women mourning from a distance.

PART V

DISCOVERY AT GOLGOTHA

Chapter 22

James studied the ominous sky.

As the outer world grew calmer, his inner world deepened with questioning thoughts.

Why was he left wounded at Gethsemane? Wasn't he worth slaying?

How did he manage to reach this destination? Wasn't he rudderless?

Who gave him the consent to stand among these brave women, who occupied Golgotha and its periphery? Wasn't he a fraud?

Righteous women.

James surveyed the foot of the hill to determine the strength in their numbers and, while doing so, he became impressed by the complexity of their feminine courage: present, unafraid, in mourning; defiant and resolute about remaining where they stood long after the Lord's body had been taken down from the wood.

He continued questioning himself without success until he was assaulted, suddenly, by an unwanted realization: he was consulting himself instead of consulting God once again.

These were *his* thoughts and not God's thoughts.

This deepened his sense of unworthiness to be standing near this hill.

"*Get away from me, Satan! You are an obstacle in my way.*"

This is how he was admonished when Jesus caught him not listening to God's thoughts. This reproach would also be directed to his brethren whenever they were not truly listening.

Peter always took this reproof harder than anybody else.

A woman's howl interrupted James's thoughts. And as he turned toward the disturbance to locate her, he heard another woman proclaim: "He was the Son of God!"

When James located her on the far side of the hill to his right, there was a man standing beside her. His profile seemed familiar, but his face was hidden within the palms of his hands.

He waited for him to reveal himself.

When the man uncovered his face, he turned away, unaware of James's presence and deeply preoccupied by his thoughts—it was Matthew.

James started to approach him when another disturbance to his left drew his attention. He recognized big Simon immediately. It appeared as if he were hunting desperately for someone.

When Simon caught sight of him, he ceased his erratic search and rushed eagerly toward him.

James responded by approaching him with equal enthusiasm.

When they met, Simon grabbed James by his upper arms and shook him affectionately. "Damn, it's good to see you."

"And you, my friend."

Simon maintained his firm hold on James and studied him at arms length. "Were you here to see him crucified?"

"No."

With relief, Simon relaxed his hold.

"Nor was I here," James added, "to see him taken down from the cross."

"I failed as well." Simon exhaled defeat. "I was a coward."

"So was I. God help me."

"God." Simon released his hold on James. "Help us all. Wherever they *all* are."

"God help us all, yes—and *you*," said James. "That's a nasty bruise on your face. What happened?"

"I abandoned my dagger."

"You did what?"

"Never mind. I'm alright." Simon touched the bruise on his face. "Are you alone?"

"Matthew is here."

"He is?" Simon's eyes brightened. "Where?"

James pointed toward a distant figure. "Over there."

"Over—ah, yes. I see. Hmm. Was . . . was he here before you?"

"I don't know. I discovered his presence just a few moments before I saw you."

"What is he doing?"

"What are you doing?"

"Damn. I deserved that."

"That was not meant to be a slight."

Simon welcomed this clarification. "I believe you."

"Look. There. Matthew seems to be lost in distant thoughts."

"I see that." Simon's sympathetic expression surrendered to the invasion of pessimism. "His thoughts won't help him."

"He doesn't know that," said James. "And neither will yours."

Simon ignored that last remark. And as he surveyed the hill behind Matthew, it occurred to him to ask, "How did you find out about . . . about *our Lord* being here?"

"A kind figure told me," said James. "Then disappeared."

Simon was perplexed. "A figure? Disappeared?"

"Yes. And you?"

"A gatekeeper at the eastern wall told me about this place."

"This. Place." James scratched his left arm. "Yes."

"Disappeared." Simon rubbed the side of his face with the knuckles of his right hand. "A kind elderly woman disappeared on me as well."

"Truly? Where?"

"Up there." Simon raised left hand and indicated the top of the hill. "When I was standing near those crosses."

"Is that who you were searching for?" James asked.

"Searching for? Ah. Yes."

"What happened?"

"I . . . I can't explain it. I . . . I don't know anything."

"Neither do I." James caught the odd expression on Simon's face. "Are you alright?"

"*No*. No." Simon took a deep breath. "Damn. I miss the freedom of being dressed in a loincloth while working on the open waters of Galilee."

"You know I always felt wet and cold and miserable on that stormy lake."

"That's your misfortune." Simon became lost within a genuine reverie. "I liked our movement upon the sea. I liked the feel of the wind."

"That wind was often violent."

"Not so violent." said Simon. "Right now, I would also take pleasure in mending my nets and repairing the boats."

"Boring work."

"I would gladly accept boredom."

"You've grown old, Simon."

"And you've grown soft."

"I wasn't soft when I had to work on the boats."

Simon rubbed the palms of his hands together. "We've grown soft."

"We're still strong," said James.

"Keeping the mobs away from our Lord didn't take much strength."

James snickered. "How quickly you forget how tired we were after a long day of crowd control. They always wanted to get too close to him, even though he spoke loudly enough to be heard by all."

"True. They always wanted to touch him. *And* they always wanted miracles."

"Yes," said James. "I admit, they always wanted something more from him."

"That's why I preferred smacking the side of any troublemaker's head when Jesus wasn't looking."

"He *was* looking. He didn't like your readiness to fight with those in the crowds."

"And I caught hell for it," said Simon.

"Don't speak so proudly."

"I speak truthfully. Be honest. It's why Jesus chose us. Besides, do you see me fighting now? Look where we are—look." Simon pointed at the crosses. "Dead. All dead."

"I'd like to think—"

"That you were smart?" Simon taunted. "You are not. You're like me—and all the rest of us!"

James grew nervous. "I think you—we're, calling attention to ourselves."

"Among women?" Simon nodded respectfully at the nearby cluster of women. "Women. Imagine that. *They* are afraid of us?" The tone of his voice reflected the irony that he felt when he repeated, "Imagine that." He rubbed his dry lips with the edge of his right index finger. "I confess, I envy them."

"But our Lord called for *us.*"

"We were *chosen* because we were big and strong and protective. Admit it. Nine of us were hard working fishermen. Nothing more."

"He had to want more than protection from us," said James. "Why was he constantly teaching us then?"

"Because he knew that we weren't keeping what he taught in our heads—or in our hearts. God help us."

"I remember what he taught us," said James.

Simon laughed. "Half the time you weren't listening—like me, like the others. And when you were, you didn't understand him."

"I understood!"

"Look who's drawing attention to us now."

James turned toward the nearby women and conveyed a sincere apology at them with a stiff bow.

"Sure," Simon taunted. "You understood our Lord. His frequent annoyance was a new kind of approval over your so-called understanding."

"You're the one who was always asking him to explain his parables." James averted his eyes from Simon. "There was plenty of annoyance there."

"And it was well earned."

James was dismayed. "Earned?"

"I did not pretend to be smart. And I believe our Lord appreciated that."

"Look at you."

"Well, he did. I think."

"Now he thinks."

"Enough to know that I am not smart. And neither are you."

"Alright, alright, it's true," James conceded. "I've never found it easy to comprehend him. And I've had a stream of headaches these last three years because of that."

"You see? There you are—you confessed. You *do* miss our past life on the lake more than you will admit."

"I won't go that far."

"All your thinking," Simon chided. "All your headaches. You're one of us."

"Stop torturing me."

"You torture *yourself*."

James was unable to respond.

"I'm sorry," said Simon. "I'll admit that our Lord gave us an easier life away from our boats—until now."

"*Now, he says!*" Matthew startled Simon and James as he stumbled toward them.

"Damn your eyes!" Simon bellowed.

"Are you alright?" James asked.

"I've been assaulted twice, then robbed," said Matthew. "I have encountered strange signs and strange women. I have been afraid, and too late in arriving here because I ran. And now, I stand before you—a complete failure. So you tell me. Am I alright?"

"You are not alone," James admitted.

Simon expressed his shame with a grunt.

"And what happened to you?" Matthew asked, referring to Simon's bruised face.

"There were bandits all along the city's wall," said Simon. "I wasn't careful. I was attacked."

"I fear none of us have been careful," said Matthew. "And the others. Where are the others? Have any of them found their way here?"

"I don't know," James answered. "But if any of the them managed to do so, they did not stay."

Simon adjusted his upper mantle. "How did *you* find out about our Lord dying on this hill?"

Matthew considered how to answer that question. "From a demon-possessed man wandering about in the Kidron Valley."

"Demon-possessed?" James repeated with interest.

"From a raving madman." Matthew emphasized. "Then I demanded to know where Jesus had been crucified."

"Crucified. How did you know about that fact?" James asked.

Matthew was perplexed. "Through the man's ravings, of course."

"Oh. I see. And?"

"I grabbed him by the front of his tunic and forced him to reveal where it happened."

"Good for you," said Simon.

"Not so good. He shook free of me and beat me into unconsciousness."

"You should have kept up your guard," Simon instructed.

"You weren't there," said Matthew. "He had the strength of a madman."

"Was he the one who robbed you of your sandals?" James inquired. "And your mantle?"

"I suppose so. I don't know." Matthew indicated his increased shame with a sigh. "I should have followed our Lord's example."

"Which one of us has?" Simon submitted.

James caught Simon's attention before he spoke. "That should not bring us any comfort."

"Comfort was not intended," Simon claimed, before he addressed Matthew. "I fully admit that it *was* bad behavior. But none of us have been able to follow our Lord's—"

"Failure. I have failed," Matthew said decisively. "I've done everything wrong. I know that. I deserved my beating." His eyes grew wide. "I'm supposed to be smart."

Simon glanced at James. "We understand that."

Matthew addressed both of them. "You do?"

"Yes," said James. "None of us have been smart."

After acknowledging James's last remark with a twisted grin, Matthew inquired, "How did *you*, and Simon, find out about our . . . our Jesus being crucified here?" He gazed at the crosses. "Up there."

"I was told by a gatekeeper," said Simon.

"A gatekeeper," Matthew repeated.

"And I was told by a kind veiled figure," said James.

"A *veiled* figure," Matthew echoed. "Who was this figure?"

"I don't know," said James. "He disappeared before I could find out who he was."

"Disappeared," Matthew emphasized. "That's odd. I encountered a beautiful women—I think."

"She was either beautiful or she wasn't," said Simon.

"Listen to me," said Matthew. "Her tunic was completely dry and immaculately clean, and her brow was smooth and clear and—she was beautiful, I tell you, and *veiled*."

"She was veiled and immaculate," Simon taunted. "Immaculate but, wait. *Wait*. I encountered an elderly woman—I think. Yes. She was elderly, and veiled."

"Where?" James asked.

"Way over there." Simon pointed at the spot where he claimed she stood.

"Where is she now?" Matthew asked.

"She disappeared," said Simon. "After she shared great wisdom with me concerning a few details about our Lord's death."

Matthew responded with wonder. "I see. *My* beautiful veiled woman also spoke with great wisdom about our Lord's death."

They both turned to James.

"*My* kind veiled figure also spoke with—wait. *Wait*." James stepped closer to them. "What is this? They all spoke about our Lord's death with great wisdom."

They were suddenly filled with wonder.

"And my veiled immaculate woman disappeared." Matthew's eyes widened. "They all disappeared."

Simon grew solemn. "All veiled. All spoke with wisdom. All disappeared."

"What has happened here?" Matthew asked.

"I don't know," James muttered. "This is a strange and disturbing discovery."

"Disturbing. Yes." Simon grabbed the front of his tunic with his right hand. "I fear that our Lord will learn what we have discovered. Learn what we have experienced. Learn what we have failed to do, and what we have said to each other during these dark hours."

"Our Lord already knows all of this," said James.

"He predicted it, as well," Matthew added with authority.

"My God," said James. "I'm frightened."

"I have been frightened for three years," Matthew admitted.

"I'll not be afraid." Simon released the hold he had on his tunic. "I won't."

"It's too late for that kind of defiance," said Matthew. "You have been uncovered, like the rest of us—no matter what you declare at this moment."

"He's right" James added. "No matter how low we whisper our guilt, I fear that our shameful behavior has been revealed."

"Our Lord warned us," Simon conceded. "I know."

Matthew circled around James and faced Simon. "The truth is, I fear our Lord. Above all."

"Be afraid," said Simon. "Go on. Be afraid."

James spread his arms with the palms of his hands facing the sky. "I fear we have lost heaven."

"The fear of heaven—lost." Matthew exhaled defeat. "We deserve that. We ran away from our Lord when fear's consequence was only death."

"The authority of damnation, and of darkness, is *His*." James's sober stance reflected the solemn tone of his voice.

"The Father. The Son." Matthew's sober tone was equal to James's. "The Divine. The Human. I don't know. Lord, my God."

"Careful there," said James. "This cloud of unknowing cannot be penetrated."

"You've seen Jesus pray," Simon submitted. "You've heard him speak to himself while on his knees. There's no divide concerning our Lord, our God."

Matthew trembled. "Do you suppose then, that we must remain within this unknowing?"

Simon spat on the ground. "What else are we to do?"

"Easy there," Matthew cautioned. "You're upsetting the women, Simon."

"The women, the women. What's a man to do at this moment?"

"Pray?" Matthew suggested. "Pray? For his forgiveness?"

Simon exhaled exasperation. "But didn't he say to us that he would always give it?"

"He did," said Matthew.

Simon grumbled with irritation. "Too much forgiveness has always made me feel uneasy."

"There can never be too much prayer," said Matthew.

"I'm talking about forgiveness," Simon insisted. "We came to expect easy forgiveness from him. And in return, we were expected to give it as easily. Our Lord has expected too much from us." He shook himself as if he were trying to shake off a flea. "The pouring out of all this forgiveness is an unreasonable demand."

"How did reason get introduced here?" Matthew stated facetiously. "Our Lord defied everything. Everything—"

"Including *my* reason," James interrupted. "Which I have always been willing to discard for him, but cannot understand why."

"Look at you!" Simon laughed. "You speak against yourself, you half-wit."

"I was *thinking*," James countered defensively.

"Big thinker," said Simon. "You're not supposed to understand why. Remember? That much I know."

"There it is again," said Matthew. "Reason. It can't be discarded."

"Our Lord said it could," Simon insisted.

"Our Lord, our Lord." Matthew was exasperated. "It was always so much easier for me to lose my reason when I was in his presence."

"His presence." Simon reached for a deep breath, then exhaled. "Yes. Somehow we must find his presence, otherwise . . . otherwise we have been fools these last three years."

"Fools you say?" Matthew shivered at that notion. "We need to quit traveling along this line of thinking."

"We're doomed, I tell you."

"Don't be so quick with that, Simon."

"James is right," said Matthew. "Second guessing our faith in him has already led us to this present road toward confusion—and damnation."

"Confusion. Bah." Simon clenched his hands into a large fist. "I won't be damned without a fight. I won't."

"Look where you are, oh brave one," James taunted. "Look."

Simon resented his sense of defeat. "Alone again. Alone!"

"Forgive us, oh Lord," James implored. "Forgive us."

"I believe we are upsetting the women once again," Matthew reported.

Simon conveyed his sincere apology to the women with a fabricated smile, accompanied by the friendly outward sweep of his right arm without a bow, before he addressed Matthew. "It's hard to speak about all of this, in the wake of what has happened, without shouting out in anger."

"We need to control ourselves," said Matthew.

"Yes, yes," Simon acquiesced.

"We have drawn too much attention to ourselves," Matthew added. "And look—those sentries up there. They have become more dissatisfied over having been assigned to this lowly duty of standing guard over executed criminals. There is no telling when they might act upon that dissatisfaction."

"That's a fine observation," said Simon. "Fortunately for us, many of those auxiliary Legionnaires are lazy mercenaries who *are* often sympathetic toward the common people."

"I agree," said Matthew. "Many of them *are* from Judea, and a few are from Galilee, but—"

"Yes, yes, I know," said Simon. "Your initial observation continues to have merit—we must remain cautious. Those mercenaries are only one measure above Jerusalem's corrupt Temple Guards—we must remain wary of them. They are not truly one of us. And because they are not sound professional Roman Legionnaires, they could easily turn violent and—well, let's not dwell on that any further. Let's be grateful for their lazy mercenary corruption."

And with that said, their following silence was invaded by more disturbing thoughts.

Chapter 23

A loud cry startled James, interrupted Matthew's self-absorption, and provoked Simon to reach inside of his tunic for a dagger that was not there.

James turned toward a distant group of agitated women as a man emerge, tall, from among them. "Look." He elbowed Matthew's left side. "Over there. Isn't that Thomas?"

"Where? Ah. Yes, it is. Thomas!"

Confusion was Thomas's initial response, then recognition when he caught sight of his brethren. He strode eagerly toward them.

"*There*. Look at him." Simon sneered with dark satisfaction. "He was hiding among those women."

"Among women. Yes. And so? You shame yourself," said Matthew. "Among women. Like us. Hiding among them here."

Simon could not respond to Matthew's reproach.

"Legionnaires," James cautioned. "Over there."

A veteran squad of Roman Legionnaires appeared from the Jerusalem side of the hill.

"Thomas! Watch out!" Simon pointed in the direction of the approaching squad.

Thomas crouched, in response to the intensity of the warning, as Matthew and Simon lowered themselves onto their right knees. After noting their response to the approaching danger, Thomas dropped slowly to his knees in an effort not to draw the squad's attention.

Late in response, James knelt beside Simon.

"The squad appears fresh and well fed and ready for violence," Simon reported.

"How do you know that?" James asked.

"Look at them. Through Damascus Gate is my guess as to where they came from. Sure. Look at them. Those are disciplined professionals. And straight from their barracks after a good night's sleep."

The Legionnaires invaded the area to enforce the power of Rome, and to prevent anyone on or near Golgotha from considering any form of protest. They were prepared to suppress any rebellion, to crush any civil disobedience.

The women responded with feminine defiance to Rome's masculine intrusion. These numerous groups of women occupied the outer foothills of Golgotha and dominated the mound itself. And as the squad marched across the hill, these groups huddled together so closely that they resembled Spartan hoplite formations prepared for battle. Their upper mantles were fastened so stiffly across the lower halves of their faces that their veils acted as face shields; their attitudes were straightened so stiffly that their presence conveyed resistance; their lamentations were so devoid of sorrow that their voices expressed contempt.

As the Legionnaires weaved passed these small phalanxes, they were amused by this harmless feminine behavior, which was usually invisible to them.

A small group of men, however, were never considered amusing, harmless, or invisible.

Three of the four disciples had veiled their faces with their upper mantles. All four had shifted furtively onto both knees and pretended to be in mourning.

Since Matthew's mantle had been stolen, he had pressed the palms of his hands together and pretended to be immersed in prayer to compensate for his unveiled face.

They inhaled fear as the Legionnaires approached them.

The Roman commander studied their submissive poses with suspicion as he and his men reached them, but he did not bring his squad to a halt.

The frightened disciples exhaled trembling after the squad continued to march pass them; they maintained their deceptive tableau until the squad left the vicinity, then they unveiled themselves.

Thomas stood up.

"That was brave of me," Simon announced.

"What should you have done?" James offered in his defense. "Fight them all with your dagger?"

Thomas approached them.

"I abandoned my dagger after I stabbed the ground of this world."

"What good did that do?" Thomas asked.

"It made me feel better," said Simon.

"Yes. Yes. I'm sure it did. But I think that was a cowardly act *as well*," Thomas asserted. "And you look as terrible as I feel."

Simon stood up. "Was that a coward's reflection, *as well*?"

Thomas hesitated before he acquiesced. "The answer is—yes. Completely a coward."

"Then you are one of us." James stood up. "I ran. I will confess to that. And so did the others here."

Everyone grumbled in shame.

"What an injured lot we are," James added.

"We *could* have fought back," said Thomas.

"*We*." James's disdain was palpable.

"Somebody *did* cut off a man's ear," Thomas offered in self defense.

Matthew was the last of them to stand up. "I don't think it was one of us who struck off that ear."

Their general agreement was mixed with uncertainty and insecurity—along with a small measure of relief.

"In fact," Matthew realized, "I believe that rabble was aching for trouble in order to justify their pleasure for violence."

"He's right," said Simon. "I wouldn't be surprised if that man was struck by one of their own on purpose."

"There you are," said Matthew. "They wanted violence. They wanted any excuse to hurt someone. Any excuse to make our Lord's arrest seem more necessary."

"Yes, yes, all true," James admitted. "But none of that matters."

"It matters to me that I denied our Lord," said Matthew.

"Don't you remember what Jesus said about belonging to him?"

Matthew was confused by James's challenge. "What did he say?"

"We belong," said James. "*We belong.*"

"Don't sidestep my thoughts about denial."

"Your thoughts are full of guilt," James continued.

"Of course they are. And so are yours." Then Matthew included Simon and Thomas. "I can hear guilt in the tone of all our voices, and see it in the expressions on our faces."

James waved the back of his right hand at Matthew. "I have freely admitted my guilt."

Matthew's barefooted stomp preceded his verbal response. "And so have I."

"Easy there you two," Thomas warned. "This is no place to have a public argument."

Each man stepped toward a common point to achieve more intimacy and to combat their insecurity.

"So fast." Simon tilted his head to the right in dismay. "It all happened so fast. That dangerous mob armed with clubs. Those Temple Guards armed with swords. They surrounded us and seized our Lord and took him away so quickly. Nobody can deny that."

"That's right," said Thomas. "There were several of us who where struck as they took our Lord away. I was one of them. See? Look at this. See? This lump on the side of my head here is proof. And there were others."

"There you are. *There*." Simon reached for a small measure of vindication. "We wanted to resist."

"But we didn't," said Matthew. "And don't be so proud of Thomas's dishonorable wound."

"I wasn't . . . ." Simon could not parry Matthew's reproof. "Yes, yes, you're right. I must admit that I ran to avoid being struck. But Peter did so as well. In fact, he was the first of us to run. I saw him."

"Bah." Thomas spat on the ground. "Peter, Peter—he's nothing."

"I wonder where he is now?" James asked.

"In denial. Like our Lord predicted," said Simon. "I'm sure of it."

"And, I believe, he is forgiven," James contended. "Somehow, I know—Jesus has forgiven him. And so, I must believe in this kind of forgiveness—our Lord's forgiveness."

Matthew raised his hands up to express his surrender. "Well. I have accepted many things during these last few years without my understanding. I will not stop now."

"I believe," said Simon. "I believe."

"So be it." Mental exhaustion overcame Thomas. "I believe. Amen. I believe."

After a long silence, each man stepped away from himself, which broke up the secure huddle that they had formed.

After another long silence, caused by the insidious growth of alienation, James shook himself free of this dark seduction and turned to Thomas. "*And you*. How did you get here?"

Thomas was puzzled by this inquiry. "I . . . I walked."

"No, no. Who told you about our Lord's crucifixion?"

"*And* that it was *here* where he died," Matthew added.

"I was led here by a potter, who possessed great wisdom," said Thomas.

"Where is he?" James inquired.

Thomas was disturbed by the question. "That's a curious thing. He disappeared."

"Ah." James glanced at Matthew, then at Simon.

Thomas noticed the change in their expressions. "What?"

"Each of us encountered someone," James began, "who either led us here or found us here. Then disappeared after explaining what happened to our Lord."

Thomas was fascinated. "And disappeared as well?"

"Yes. After interpreting our Lord's death," Matthew repeated.

"Interpreting. Yes. Of *that* I received a lot of," said Thomas. "And in my dreams as well."

"What do you mean by that?" Simon asked.

"I encountered this potter in my dreams, then discovered him sitting beside me when I woke up."

"Now that's a story for you," said Simon.

"It's the truth," Thomas insisted.

"I believe I speak for all of us here when I say, we believe you," said James.

The other men nodded in agreement.

Thomas scratched the back of his left hand. "So, what does this mean, I wonder?"

"That kind figure who spoke to me in Jerusalem," said James, "freely gave me milk and bread and comfort and—it was a gift."

"Kind figure?" Thomas asked.

"And that beautiful immaculate woman who spoke to me," Matthew claimed, "freely cleansed my spirit and gave me courage. It was as if she were empowered by—by something holy."

"Immaculate woman," Thomas muttered without understanding.

"Well, it was an elderly woman, who put me in my place with ease by—by her spirit." Simon was dismayed. "How was that possible?"

Thomas cleared his throat. "I'm not sure that I understand any of this. But that veiled potter who spoke to *me*, somehow, and freely, empowered me to go on believing. It was as if a strong force had come upon me."

"*Veiled* you say?" Simon queried.

"Yes," Thomas asserted. "A veiled potter."

"They were all veiled," said Matthew.

"That's interesting," said Thomas. "All?"

"My veiled figure," said James. "Matthew's veiled immaculate woman. And Simon's veiled elderly woman. All."

"That's amazing." Thomas pressed the palm of his right hand against his chin. "But I don't understand any of this."

"It seems as if," James added, "as if each of those who we met were more than . . . than, they seemed to be—what?"

"Filled with a spirit?" Matthew ventured to say.

"Wait." James was struck by a sudden realization. "Dare we say—with the Holy Spirit?"

"My God." Matthew was astonished. "That must have been the source of their wisdom. What else could it have been?"

"That seems right," said Simon. "It was as if my elderly woman understood me. She certainly did not fear me like so many women do."

"That's because . . . ." James looked to Matthew for reassurance. "Could it be?"

Matthew eyes brightened. "We have witnessed the Holy Spirit descend upon our Lord, haven't we?"

Thomas was wonder-struck. "But is that what *we* experienced?"

"I don't know. *My* experience was certainly not the same as our Lord's experience with the Holy Spirit." Simon rubbed his forehead. "But I am no longer the same man. That much I know."

"Present. Then not present." Then Matthew suggested, "I think my veiled immaculate woman was empowered by the Holy Spirit."

"That would explain a lot," Simon agreed. "My veiled elderly woman must have been empowered as well."

The other two agreed that they were also visited by those who must have been empowered by the Holy Spirit.

"But yet, what happened?" James wondered. "In the end, it was so—so ordinary."

"And then it was not," said Matthew.

They traded nods of understanding about what could not be fully understood. And somehow, at that moment, they accepted what little that could be understood.

"What do we do now?" Simon asked.

"Do?" Thomas's expression soured unexpectedly. "I don't know." His tone grew caustic. "But I do know that the Holy Spirit did not visit Judas, because of what, wait— *what's* happened to him? Where has *he* gone? Has anyone seen him?"

"I have," said James.

"Where?"

"In Jerusalem. During the night."

"That betrayer." Simon fueled the bitterness that Thomas had ignited. "That traitor."

They gathered together to share their hostility, to contain its growth, and to keep their dark opinions a secret.

Chapter 24

Thomas released a harsh curse before he turned away from the tight pack of indignant men. "Judas."

"We must try to forget him," said Matthew.

"We must try to forgive him," James suggested.

Thomas cleared his throat. "How are we going to do that?"

"We have to," James urged. "Somehow."

"I don't know anything about our Lord's forgiveness. I don't know how it works." Thomas struggled with these notions for a moment, then conceded. "Alright, so we must forgive Judas. But I . . . I don't know how." His gaze shifted from James to Matthew. "Forgive. Forget. Alright. I'll agree with *you*, Matthew—yes—forget him. Alright, alright. But I think, well—we, yes, *we* need to let this go—for now." He peered at Simon. "Because, I believe it's more important to think about what we need to do now—for ourselves. Right?"

"I agree." Simon stepped away from where he stood.

"But don't we also need to find out what has happened to the others?" James asked.

"Arrested. In hiding. Or dead," said Matthew. "We will know soon enough."

"He's right," Simon added. "And so is Thomas. We need to think about what we are going to do now."

"We better leave this place before we are arrested," said Matthew. "That squad of Legionnaires won't march across this hill a second time without interrogating us. But one question remains. Go where?"

"Good question," said Simon. "I don't know."

"I'll take you to safety," a woman volunteered.

She startled them all into a brief moment of silence.

With the tip of his right forefinger, Matthew wiped away a speck of dirt from the inner corner of his left eye before he stepped toward her. "Who are you?"

"A disciple of our Lord—like you." She glanced at Thomas. "And you." Then at Simon. "And you."

"We don't know you," said James.

The woman ignored his concern. "I am offering all of you food and shelter as well."

James glanced at Matthew, then at the others—together, they murmured a willingness to go with her.

A reluctant smile escaped from the right corner of James's mouth before he addressed her. "I think we all agree. We will go with you to—"

"Where?" Thomas intervened.

With the slight gesture of her right hand, she indicated the direction. "Into Jerusalem." Then invited them all to follow her with a left-handed gesture before she turned away from them and started walking.

And so, with the collective courage of having nothing to lose, they followed this professed woman disciple toward an unknown destination within Jerusalem, toward an unknown shelter that offered some promise of comfort and safety.

PART VI

THE WOMEN AND SAFETY

Chapter 25

They followed her into Jerusalem's second quarter by entering the city through its Damascus Gate. Then they traveled along the edge of the Tyropoeon Valley across the second quarter, journeyed passed the wealthy upper city, and entered the poor southern region of the lower city—a district crowded with small limestone houses.

The lower city was densely populated with the indigent, the unemployed, the disabled, the criminal, and the underpaid worker of the lower-class. This was a place of true poverty and squalor, of serious crime and violence, and of desperate hunger and homelessness.

It was into this squalid and unfamiliar world that this proud woman, this alleged disciple of Jesus, bravely guided four troubled men through a dangerous labyrinth of foul smelling narrow streets and alleyways to their destination.

A beige upper mantle, which matched her full length woolen tunic, covered this woman's hair, lower face, and neck. By the brightness of her eyes and the smoothness of her brow, she appeared to be young. The cloth belt tied snugly around her waist revealed a slight figure. Her feminine bearing was formal—straight-backed, level-headed, and sure-footed. Her steady gait was youthfully light upon feet that were protected by thin leather sandals. The lower portion of her tunic seemed to billow, like a sail, behind her as if she were walking against a stern wind. But there was no air flow of in this vicinity.

After turning right at a crossroad and entering another midsized thoroughfare, the young woman pointed ahead at a modest dwelling to indicate their destination. It was a humble, two story dwelling. Its outside stone stairway led to a second floor doorway.

The limestone houses that crowded the length of the avenue were similar in construction. And the adjacent alleyways to several of these homes were cluttered with refuse, which caused discomfort to the inhabitants with its foul odor.

When they reached the dwelling, they entered it through a wooden door on the first floor and proceeded toward the rear of the residence.

The interior of the ground floor was plain and orderly. There were three living areas that were defined by walls with very large archways. So large, in fact, that the separating walls were mere demarcations between these rooms.

The front room was a domestic storage space with supply cupboards, water vessels, food bins, herb boxes, oil jars, wine skins, spare oil lamps, grain hand-mills, and a variety of clay pots and jars, pitchers and dishes, as well as baskets, leather buckets, and rolled up reed mats. In addition, several chickens wandered about freely.

The center room was an elevated common living area with stools, benches, and a large table. In this room, the inhabitants washed and ate and relaxed from their day of work. The three-foot elevation provided a stone quarter-wall, which extended across the entire lower portion of the separating archway to discourage the animals that were being sheltered in the front storage space from entering the central living quarters.

The back bedroom was on the same level as the center living room. There were three beds: a large master bed to the left and two single beds on the opposite side of the room. The beds consisted of padded mattresses spread on top of low-built wooden bed platforms. The mattresses appeared to be clean and comfortable. A lamp-stand, with a lit oil lamp, stood near the large master bed in this windowless room.

The young woman approached the glowing oil lamp, removed it from the lamp-stand, and went to a wooden ladder. She stepped onto the bottom rung with her left foot, turned to the weary men, and said, "Follow me."

So they followed her up the ladder, single file, and passed through an open trapdoor that led to a second floor bedroom.

After she stepped into the room, the young woman stood by the trapdoor, waited for them to pass through, then lowered the door. She walked toward the center of the room and revealed its contents with the oil lamp.

The upstairs bedroom was furnished with half-a-dozen, single bed mattresses that were spread directly on the floor—the head of three mattresses were placed against the right wall, and the other three mattresses were similarly placed on the opposite wall on the left. Evidently, this barracks style arrangement was designed to accommodate as many guests as possible.

"Make yourselves comfortable. It will be safe here." She waited for the them to disperse and claim a bed mattress.

Each weary man chose a corner bed. Matthew sat down on his mattress and the others stood by theirs.

She approached a table located at the center of the room and placed the oil lamp upon it. The table was set with two loaves of bread, a bowl of figs, and two large wine flasks with several cups orbiting the flasks.

"Eat. Remain here. I will be back." She approached the trapdoor, opened it, and stepped onto the top rung of the ladder.

"When will that be?" James asked.

"Tomorrow." She shut the trapdoor as she descended the ladder.

"She doesn't reveal a lot," said Matthew.

Thomas approached the table. "No matter." He poured himself a cup of wine.

Simon expressed relief. "At least we're safe."

"For now. I hope." Thomas drank deeply. "Hmm. Good wine." He sat on the matted floor beside the table and poured himself more wine.

Simon joined him at the table, plucked a fig from the bowl, and bit into it as he sat beside Thomas. "Hmm. Hungry." He grabbed one of the loaves and broke it.

Thomas poured wine into another cup and offered it to Simon.

As Simon and Thomas ate and drank in earnest, James approached Matthew, who continued to sit on the corner mattress that he had claimed. As soon as he sat beside Matthew, he whispered, "What do you think we should do?"

Matthew scratched the left side of his head. "There's nothing we can do but wait. It'll be dark soon and—well, I don't know. I'm too tired to go on right now."

"I agree. Our Lord's crucifixion has left me empty. And I continue to feel exposed by our hateful thoughts toward Judas."

"Our Lord's death has left me empty as well," Matthew whispered. "And as for Judas, I feel bad as well."

"Truly?"

"Yes." Matthew frowned. "Our hateful exchange concerning Judas before we left Golgotha has also left me feeling exposed."

"Exposed," James repeated. "I fear that our dark thoughts can never remain a secret. I wish we hadn't done that."

"I agree. Sadly, all our combined curses against Judas did not succeed in uncovering forgiveness toward him."

"I know, I know. We failed again."

Matthew clenched his hands together and pressed his doubled fist against his chest. "What possessed Judas to betray our Lord, I wonder? Satan?"

"Perhaps. But you would think that after being possessed by our Lord," James murmured, "that Satan or any evil spirit or dark power or . . . or *any* sinister force or entity would not have been able to possess him. How was that possible?"

"Aren't we on the edge of a dark power as well?"

James was appalled. "Hold your tongue."

"Hold yours. Judas was one of us. No more. No less."

"Then . . . then it could have been me instead of Judas."

Matthew trembled. "It could have been any one of us. Yes."

"That's a strange truth." James shifted uneasily on the mattress. "I'm not wanting to understand this."

"On the edge. Remember? We are always on the edge."

James averted his eyes from Matthew's. "His betrayal could not have been premeditated. I knew him."

"And you did not like him." Matthew nudged James with his elbow. "Do not pretend otherwise."

"I tried." James straightened his back. "Look here. We got along."

"Calm down." Matthew glanced at Simon and Thomas. "Don't be so loud. You'll aggravate those two."

James pressed his right hand over his mouth and peered at his hardy brethren, who were enjoying their food and wine. "Sorry."

"Don't go strange on me."

"But you're twisting my thoughts."

"Remember, our Lord chose him to be one of us," said Matthew.

"Why does that make me feel more uneasy?"

"Because, I think, each one of us is a little like him."

James scowled. "Like Judas?"

"Shh." Matthew glanced at the other two, but they were enjoying the effects of the wine. "We're always near the edge of taking a fall."

"That doesn't make any sense."

"That's the frightening part of being a man," Matthew warned. "Not knowing the why or the when, of the next fall."

"Like Judas," James muttered. "Poor Judas."

Matthew nodded. "What a fall."

"From our Lord."

"The longest fall of all."

An uncomfortable passage of time deepened Matthew's last remark.

Thomas grunted as he poured wine into his cup. "You two over there are sounding like a couple of old women. Get off that mattress and join us. The food is good."

"And so is the wine." Simon wiped his mouth with the back of his hand and offered James what was left in his cup. "Here. You better take a drink before Thomas and I finish this wine."

James approached Simon, sat at the table, and accepted Simon's cup. He drank deeply. "You're right. This is good."

Simon grabbed one of the flasks and poured another cup for himself as Matthew joined them at the table. But when he caught hold Matthew's longing eyes, he surrendered the cup to him.

Matthew drank half the wine, then grabbed the untouched loaf and sniffed the bread. "Hmm. Fresh."

Simon poured himself another cup. "Does anybody here have any objections to my drinking this one?"

James laughed, then Thomas, and then—they all laughed for the first time since . . . since long before their last supper.

They tore into the second loaf of bread and they devoured the figs and they drank all the wine. They almost forgot that they were in trouble.

Then they grew somber and quiet after the food and the wine took full effect on their weary bodies and souls. Their prolonged silence lasted longer than the amount of oil that was left in the lamp.

"What do we do now?" Matthew asked.

"Let's get some sleep," Simon answered.

"Yes. Sleep," Thomas agreed.

"It's too dark to do anything else," James reasoned.

"And she told us to remain here," said Matthew.

"Great." Thomas crawled toward the wall at the head of his corner mattress and leaned against it. "We've been reduced to taking orders from a woman."

The creeping passage of time, accompanied by the injuries that were sustained during the previous night and day, softened Thomas and the others.

As time expanded, they were seduced into believing in the relative safety of the present. Then fatigue presented itself and demanded their attention.

Slumber triumphed over all of them.

PART VII

NIGHTMARES AND DREAMS

Chapter 26

The upward thrust of Simon's dagger into the man's abdomen was so powerful that he knew the tip of the blade had penetrated the bottom of the victim's heart. The man gasped, then fell to the ground after Simon pulled out the dagger.

Simon knelt beside him and plunged the dagger into his chest.

He stabbed the man repeatedly.

The berserk stabbings continued—head, thighs, abdomen—until Simon grew tired of mutilating the body.

Simon wiped the dagger clean against the dead man's tunic, then stood up.

He inserted the dagger into its sheath, which hung from his neck by a leather halter-strap—all hidden inside of his tunic.

He laughed until he became breathless—then afraid.

Simon turned away from his dark self, opened his eyes, and encountered the bright eyes of the veiled elderly woman he had met on Golgotha.

She stood before him.

"You again." Simon was too exhausted by his nightmare to be astonished.

"Yes. This is not reality."

"I had a bad dream."

"And now you will have a good one," the veiled elderly woman pledged.

"Bah." Simon sat up.

"You should avoid a hard heart."

"Don't cast our Lord's thoughts upon me," he asserted. "I'm not worthy."

"Why do you doubt so hard?"

"Woman. Haven't you ever run away? Haven't you ever hidden?"

"Not from *His* truth."

Simon groused. "Beautiful."

"It's the truth."

"It's *my* fault that I ran."

"Don't judge yourself." The veiled elderly woman softened her tone. "Along what path do you stand now?"

Simon scratched his forehead. "I don't know."

"And still, you have the courage to judge yourself."

"Courage! Listen to you. Courage." He slammed his right fist into the palm of his left hand. "I'm simply admitting that I am a failure." He pulled his left hand away from his right. "I know that the seed of our Lord's message has fallen upon the rocky ground of my faith—where I am right now. I admit that I have lost his message, that my heart is empty, that my belief in him has flattened. I am lost."

"He spoke of Satan," she offered.

"There you are again."

"He *did*."

"Satan. Fine. Alright. So he did."

"You see?"

"See what?" Simon exhaled resentment. "It was not my fault that our Lord was arrested?" He came close to tears. "I was always glad to be with him."

"You have not failed any test."

A long and troubled silence separated them.

"Do you think our Lord knows what I'm feeling? What I'm doing?" Simon asked.

She placed the palm of her right hand over the back of her left. "He predicted it."

"Are you sure it was me and my brethren that Jesus was speaking about?"

"Yes. You, like the others at the supper table, denied him."

"So I did."

"And now look at you. You're hiding from yourself as if it will not be brought out into the light," she said.

"Into the light." Simon peered at the sky. "Oh, that fearful light—"

"Will dim—"

"God help me. Please. I am nothing. Nothing."

"*That* is something," she said.

He rebelled against her gentle authority. "Small comfort. A woman's comfort."

She disarmed his bitter remark. "I will not argue with a nothing."

Simon was taken aback by her statement. "You make me feel ashamed. Like my Lord often did."

"How could that be? He spoke to you with great care."

"I know that!" His tone became more desperate with his increasing anguish. "He kept telling me not to worry about getting the food I needed to stay alive, or about getting the food I needed to provide for my . . . *my* neglected family, damn it."

"Our Lord became angry with you," she recalled.

"Of course he did. I had little faith, he told me."

"He was always saying that."

"*Women.*" Simon sought her eyes. "He also said that my wife had greater faith than I."

"He was always different about women. You saw that."

Her statement annoyed him. "And I heard it as well. He always gave our women more credit than they deserved. I never understood that."

"There was always a bigger message behind the meaning in his words," she reminded him.

"Then explain the message behind those words to me," he challenged. "Because whenever I think about the impractical spirit of his message, when I'm not in his presence, confusion reigns within me."

"Then remain in his presence," she replied.

"How?" Simon demanded.

"The Lord has always provided for you."

"Where are his provisions now? I need them."

"What has he done for me now? Is that it?"

"Don't be righteous with me. You're pulling your thin cloak closer to your frail body because of the cold emptiness surrounding you—like me." Simon tamped the dirt that he was sitting on with the tips of his fingers. "This damp ground beneath me here has penetrated your aching bones as well, old woman." He became aware of her active silence. "Why hasn't the Holy Spirit provided me with an answer?"

Her eyes brightened.

Simon pointed his right forefinger at her. "Slippery. You are very slippery."

Her dignified silence made Simon feel uncomfortable.

"I . . . I don't understand the Holy Spirit," he continued. "There. I have said it."

Again, no response from her.

"Where is your Kingdom, my Lord?" Simon reclined, feeling exhausted. "I'm sorry. I know I must believe that my Lord provides." Simon covered his eyes with the palms of his hands. "I'm desperate for spiritual provisions."

The veiled elderly woman spoke from a distance. "His truth will prevail. Have faith in Jesus. Trust in him. That's all you need to know."

"And I'm sorry for releasing all my doubts upon you." He removed his hands from his eyes to look at her, but she was gone.

Simon sat up from where he had been asleep. The upper portion of his tunic was soaked with perspiration.

He caught his breath. He caught sight of the others who were also awake or had been awakened by—

Chapter 27

Matthew inserted his reed pen into the bronze inkwell that was located on the upper right corner of his accounting table, then wiped off the ink that blackened the tips of his first two fingers and thumb on a folded hand towel. He slumped against the table, momentarily, then straightened up on the bench that he was sitting on before he leaned back against the stone wall behind him.

He glanced at his right hand and grimaced. The oily soot-stain that always remained on his fingers reminded him of his loathsome occupation—a tax collector. He spent the entire day perched on this hard bench demanding more money, arguing about Rome's legal authority, and threatening property seizure.

The rear of the sackcloth canopy overhead was permanently secured to the stone wall. And the front edge of the coarse cloth was secured at both corners onto a pair of rough hewed posts that were impaled into the ground and structurally reinforced at their bases with an odd assortment of stones and broken bricks. The canopy provided shade and definition to this temporarily appropriated booth for the official use of Rome.

Matthew folded his hands together and rested them on the accounting table, which was crowded with scrolls and purses full of coin: Jewish, Greek, Roman, Persian; bronze, copper, silver, gold. He closed his eyes and took a moment to appreciate the end of this miserable day. To his disappointment, however, someone shuffled into this crude booth and approached his table.

Matthew opened his eyes and studied the peasant farmer who stood humbly before him.

The man's knee-length tunic was tidy, but threadbare, and cinched at the waist with a cloth belt. He wore a clean square of wool on his head that was held in place by a double wrap of cloth tied in the back. His beard was trimmed, his eyes were troubled. "I can't afford to pay you what," he peered at Matthew's Roman assistant, "what he says that I owe Rome."

Matthew glanced at one of the unrolled scrolls on the table. "And you are . . . ?"

"Benjamin, the son of Heber."

Matthew snatched the pen from the inkwell and used it as a guide to scan the list of names on the scroll. "Ah. Yes. Here it is." He marked the name. "You owe nine minas."

The peasant farmer's lips trembled. "But that—"

"Includes your back taxes as well," the Roman assistant interjected.

"Galen. Please." Matthew raised his pen toward his assistant to emphasize that he wanted to handle this man by himself.

Benjamin bit his lower lip. "But how can my family survive without—?"

"You heard him," said Galen. "Nine minas."

Matthew was annoyed with his Roman assistant's interference and conveyed his displeasure with a frown.

Benjamin leaned over Matthew's table and stated, "I have thirty-eight shekels. That's all I have. Even if I were to sell—"

"That's four hundred and twelve shekels short," was Matthew's cold response.

The man shivered at Matthew's heartlessness. "Even if I were to sell everything of value, everything that I have, every—"

"Last time," Galen interrupted. "You owe a full four-hundred-and-fifty shekels. Pay it or forfeit your land in three days."

Benjamin pressed his hands together. "Please. You . . . you're one of us. My family will starve in the countryside. They will—"

"Pay or starve." Matthew avoided the man's eyes as he placed the pen beside the scroll. "That is not my concern."

Benjamin lowered his hands to his side. "You are asking me for . . . for the moon." He turned around to seek sympathy from a brethren. But he forgot that he had been the last man standing outside awaiting his fate. He was alone and desperate.

Matthew rolled up the scroll that contained the farmer's tax debt. "Get out." He nodded at Galen to have him usher out the man.

Benjamin knelt before the indifferent tax collector. "Please. Have mercy on me and my—"

"Get out!" Galen grabbed the peasant farmer by the back of his tunic and forced him to rise. "You have three days. No more."

"Three more seasons would not—"

"Be here in three days with full payment or you'll be visited by either Roman Legionnaires or by Herod's Guards."

"Please."

"They will not be as patient with you then, as we have been with you now," said the Roman assistant.

Benjamin's expression hardened before he addressed Matthew with disdain. "Publican. Traitor."

Matthew avoided eye contact with him. "Get him out of here, Galen." He turned away from Benjamin to avoid witnessing the manner in which his Roman assistant escorted Benjamin out of the booth.

Galen yawned when he returned. "Well, my friend, this has been another long day."

Matthew placed his elbows on the table and pressed his forehead against the heels of his hands. "They all seem long these days." He rubbed his forehead with the palms of his hands, then grabbed the edge of the table and pushed himself back against the stone wall. "Heavy handed. You're always pressing me to be more heavy handed than I already am."

"You can't be soft with these people."

"I know, I know," Matthew lamented.

"Remember," Galen emphasized. "It's no concern of yours if these people can't afford to pay their taxes."

"You're right." Matthew stood up to emphasize his renewed determination. "I can't be concerned about extorting what we need."

"That's right." Galen smiled. "Good man. Remember, we have to make a living. Good man."

Matthew walked passed Galen, approached the edge of the canopy's shade, and studied the village's only road. "I don't need compliments."

The lane was rutted, and the poor dwellings were tightly packed along its length. Two scavenger dogs crossed the southern end of the road after investigating the garbage that had been thrown out.

The village felt abandoned because its inhabitants had made an effort not to be seen by the publican and his Roman assistant.

The odor of burnt dung hung in the air. There was no marketplace here.

"You and your guilt." Galen turned away from Matthew, approached the table, then sat on the bench. "Damn. It feels good to sit down. At our next village, it's your turn to manage the long line." He took off his right sandal and massaged his foot. "You're not going to discover anything out there. You won't see yourself. Those are not your people."

"My people?" Then he repeated cynically, "My people."

"I'm your people." Galen slipped on his sandal. "We're a lot alike."

"Sure. A Roman like you and a Judean like me are . . . are . . . ."

"Corrupt. There." Galen took off his left sandal. "I'm not afraid to say it."

Matthew turned to Galen. "Yes."

"I'm not afraid to admit who we are." Galen massaged his left foot. "Thieves like us transcend all races—all tribes. All. And taxes will always make our kind rich."

Matthew nodded. "I need a drink."

"Don't feel so bad about being bad, my friend."

Matthew turned toward the sun-baked village and watched a man, who suddenly appeared, guide his over-burdened ass along the road. "Those people will starve when we—"

"Can't be concerned about that." Galen slipped on his sandal and stood up.

"You Romans have it easy," said Matthew. "My friend, I have to consider God, and what God will—"

"Stop. Stop. I have more Gods to worry about than you do." Galen chuckled. "*One God.*" He approached the edge of the canopy's shade, stood alongside Matthew, and peered at the impoverished village. "You and your people." He shook his head dismissively. "It's ridiculous, even sacrilegious, to be worried about only one God."

Matthew went back to the table, placed the palms of his hands upon it, then leaned forward in response to his weariness after closing his eyes. "One God. Yes. One God."

He turned away from his dark self, opened his eyes, and encountered the bright eyes of the veiled immaculate woman he had met on Golgotha.

She stood before him.

"You again." Matthew was too exhausted by his nightmare to be astonished.

"Yes. This is not reality."

"I had a bad dream."

"And now you will have a good one," the veiled immaculate woman pledged.

"Sure, sure," was Matthew's cynical response. "And I must be the greatest among my fellow disciples."

"Why would you say that?"

"Because I have fallen the hardest. I was a heartless tax collector who robbed his people—in the name of Rome." And with a self-satisfied tone in his voice, he added, "Therefore, I have become the least worthy of us all."

"I believe Judas deserves that honor."

"Judas!"

"He must be the greatest," she said.

"Judas was—yes. There is Judas."

"He has certainly become the least and, therefore, the greatest among those who have abandoned the Lord."

"The greatest," Matthew repeated. "Fallen and abandoned and . . . ." He grinned sardonically. "Then . . . then I must be getting close to being the greatest—"

"Not—close at all," she said.

Matthew attempted to shift the subject away from himself. "Alright. Our Lord must have known about what

Judas planned to do. I saw their last moments together before Judas left our supper table."

"You saw, you saw," she mimicked. "Judas is the greatest among you."

"That declaration leaves me empty."

"I have taken away your false magnitude of guilt."

Matthew was vexed. "Is that the truth?"

"Believe in the Lord," she answered softly. "That's all you have to do."

"Yet it remains: I have failed him."

"He knew you would."

"So then, is everything foretold?"

"Yes. And no."

"That leaves me confused."

"I know."

The silence between them intensified Matthew's introspection. "So, Jesus knew that everybody would fail him."

"That's right," she said.

Matthew reached into his memory. "Alright, it's true. Many of the Judean authorities would not receive our Lord as he made his way toward Jerusalem with us this last time." He nibbled on his lower lip. "Could it be that they were no longer willing to tolerate this . . . this Galilean?" He raised his right hand to help qualify himself. "That was *their* perception of the Lord, not mine."

"I understand. But once again, you must continue to remember: our Lord knew that everybody would fail him; and our Lord knew that he was going to be handed over to the authorities by—"

"Judas, again!" Matthew interrupted. "There you are."

"Judas was nothing. He was a mere instrument. Again, our Lord was always going to be handed over to the Chief Priest, and then to Pilate. You and the ordinary people on the streets and in the countryside could not alter that."

"Those crowds of ordinary people, who supposedly believed in Jesus, went along with the wishes of their enemy," Matthew submitted.

"Those ordinary people, who believed in Jesus, were powerless. They did not approve of his treatment. But they were nothing to the authorities. You, of all people, should understand that lack of power."

"Yes, yes." Matthew groaned. "I, a heartless tax collector, would know."

"The people have no power against Rome," she maintained.

"But many of those same people gave our Lord to Caiaphas, then to Pilate, and—"

"Those who had fallen. Those who never believed. Those who were the mercenary mob. *Those* were the few, not the many. *They* were not the many."

"But those few also heard the Lord directly. How could they not have comprehended some of his words?"

"You heard him," she said. "But look at yourself now. Where are you?"

Matthew was surprised by her question. "Yes. Yes. And I am ashamed. The Good News was offered to the people by our Lord—just like me." Then he rose to his self-defense. "But most of them had nothing to lose but their hunger by listening to him." He slapped his chest with his right hand. "It was me and my brethren disciples who were in true jeopardy." He wagged his right hand at her. "Don't forget their hunger. Jesus often gave them bread: their reward for listening to him; their compensation for spending time with him; their restitution for the losses they could incur by being monitored by the Legionnaires."

She folded her hands together to exhibit her patience. "Love has such a small price. Don't you think so?"

Matthew did not know how to respond to her.

"These corrupt and clever leaders do not demand any price," she continued. "They simply want absolute obedience to *them*, and not to *God*. In other words, *they want everything*."

He acknowledged that fact. "And so, there it is—our people comply."

"They have no choice. It has been the only way they know how to save themselves from harm," she said. "That is, until now."

"Until Jesus, you mean."

"That's right," she said. "Jesus."

"Why hasn't the Holy Spirit provided me with an answer?"

"Hold onto your belief in Jesus," she urged.

"Hold onto him." The tone of Matthew's voice revealed his continued internal struggle. "Is that all I need to do?"

"Believe in him."

He turned away from her and folded his hands over his eyes. "I feel emptier now than when I thought I was the greatest of them all."

The veiled immaculate woman spoke from a distance. "Have faith in Jesus. Trust in him. That's all you need to know."

Matthew unfolded his hands from his eyes. "I understand. I think." He turned to her, but she was gone.

Matthew sat up from where he had been asleep—his neck hurt. The upper portion of his tunic was soaked with perspiration. He caught his breath. He caught sight of the others who were also awake or had been awakened by—

Chapter 28

Thomas slammed his right fist into the palm of his left hand. "I don't believe you. I won't. I won't!"

"I'm telling you the truth," said the short man with a high-pitched voice. "Jesus fed that large crowd of people after he healed the sick."

"I have to admit, I was not there that time, but—"

"Five loaves of bread and two fishes was all Jesus had available." The man was powerfully built.

Thomas placed the palms of his hands over his ears. "Yes! I heard about these few loaves and fishes. I heard!"

The top of the man's bald head glistened with perspiration; his upper mantle had fallen to his shoulders. "I swear to you, he fed a whole countryside full of people at the end of that day."

"Stop it. Stop it!" Thomas grabbed the man by the front of his tunic. "Liar."

"I don't have a cock in this fight. I'm not a disciple."

Thomas released the man's tunic and pushed him away. "Damn your eyes."

"Why are you so angry?"

"Five loaves of bread. Two little fishes. Too many peo-ple." Thomas was consumed with indignation. "I wasn't there. Damn. I missed it. I always missed understanding his miracles. Why? Why!"

"How is this to be understood?"

"Don't humor me."

The man pouted. "I don't know what to say. But I bit into real bread. I swear. What you've heard is real. What I've told you is true!"

"What I've heard. What you've told me. *I am* one of his disciples! *I'm* supposed to hear—*I'm* the one to tell you! Or someone like you!"

"This is not my fault. The truth is—"

"Not, to be understood!" Thomas grabbed the dumb-founded man by his upper arms. "What is truth? What is real? I'll show you real!" Thomas released the man's left arm, grabbed its freed forearm, and bit it.

"Damn!" The man pulled away from Thomas and punched him in the gut with a hard right. "You are pos-sessed!" Then he struck Thomas's jaw with a left jab. "You—you filthy cur!"

Thomas staggered sideways as he pressed the side of his jaw with the palm of his right hand. "Yes. I'm a *mad* dog!"

The angry man placed his hand over his bitten fore-arm as he backed away from this demon-possessed being.

After dropping to his knees, Thomas fell forward on his hands, then crawled toward the short man's feet. "*I am* a dog!"

The man placed his right foot on Thomas's left shoulder and pushed him aside. Then he laughed hysterically at Thomas before he walked away.

Thomas collapsed upon the ground, rolled onto his back, and howled before he closed his eyes.

He turned away from his dark self, opened his eyes, and encountered the bright eyes of the veiled potter, who had accompanied him for part of the way when he was plodding toward Golgotha.

"You again." Thomas was too exhausted by his nightmare to be astonished.

"Yes. This is not reality."

"I had a bad dream."

"And now you will have a good one," the veiled potter pledged.

"Bah. What's different? Our Lord rebuked our teachers of the law. But I am no better than them. I have washed my clothes, but my body remains dirty."

"You must do the best you can."

Thomas sat up. "Then you understand my meaning?"

"Everyone is a sinner. The law makes that very clear."

"He told me to be on my guard against that law," said Thomas. "It could not put me right with God."

"Jesus told you many things. Did you understand him?"

"You see me hiding here, don't you?" Thomas could not conceal his shame. "I listened. But I never understood. What's wrong with me?"

"I don't know," said the veiled potter. "The Lord's will does not always bring peace."

"Always—never."

There was no response.

"I served him for years," said Thomas, "and look at me—I continue to hold onto the tomb of narrow observances. Look at me. I'm hopeless, now that he is no longer with me."

"I thought you were on the road to facing yourself."

"Not voluntarily," said Thomas. "My hopelessness has always appeared as soon as my Lord wasn't present."

"I see."

"The truth is, I never fully gave myself to him. I pretended to be someone other than myself in order to . . . to—*I pretended.*"

"You worked hard."

"All show and tell. There was no truth in it." Thomas sighed. "Why hasn't the Holy Spirit provided me with an answer?"

Thomas reclined onto the ground and peered into the dark, then closed his eyes before he spoke with resignation. The tone in his voice conveyed finality. "I have not been fully with him." He exhaled exasperation. "I do not like this constant looking at myself."

The veiled potter spoke from a distance. "Then stop looking at yourself. Have faith in Jesus. Trust in him. That's all you need to know."

"There is no peace on earth, I think." When Thomas opened his eyes, the veiled potter was gone.

Thomas sat up where he had been asleep. He touched the blood clotted lump on his head with his left hand and winced—his head continued to throb from that hard blow he had received at Gethsemane. He caught his breath. He caught sight of the others who were also awake or had been awakened by—

Chapter 29

"You abandoned your family!"

James wanted to hit his brother-in-law, but he resisted. "You have no right to say that to me. *And* you have no right to judge me."

"It's what I believe."

"I am immune to your contempt."

"Are you immune to the fact that your wife has turned her back on you forever? She has come to hate you."

James glared at him. "That can't be helped."

"My sister believes that you have sacrificed your family for—for what?"

"They are not living without the things they need," said James. "They are not suffering. They have food and shelter and clothing."

"Don't walk away from me. You are detested!"

"I don't care!"

"You are a social outcast, a renegade from our people's faith—an enemy of the true Messianic hope."

"Those are my father's words," said James.

"Those are patriotic words spoken by a devout man."

"He is wrong."

"He is your father," his brother-in-law said with ferocity. "And he has remained loyal to the cause."

"Cause. What cause?"

"The true cause against Rome."

James scoffed. "A lost cause."

"No. We are an occupied land."

"Yes. We are a conquered people," said James.

"Alright, alright." His brother-in-law exhaled disgust. "To surrender to a powerful enemy is one thing. But to surrender yourself to an itinerant sorcerer who publicly displays affection toward women and who—"

"Jesus. His name is Jesus."

His brother-in-law gasped. "Listen to you."

"His name! Say it!"

"You've been disloyal to God. And your allegiance has fallen outside the boundaries of our society, and—"

"Forgiven." James clenched his teeth. "All is forgiven— Jesus has said."

"Has said, has said—*you*, you always have strange and repulsive answers. You're nothing but a sinner."

James approached him. "Yes. I abandoned my home. I abandoned my tribe. I abandoned the old faith. I know your sister believes that I have ruined her reputation. But—" He lost the intensity of his anger. "You should have listened to Jesus."

"I did!" His brother-in-law spat on the ground with contempt. "He is nothing but a magician, I tell you! Your Jesus cannot save you now."

James was startled by that remark.

"That's right. You heard me clearly. You are a sinner—a real sinner. Always. You cannot be saved. And I don't want you to ever forget that."

James punched him in the jaw.

His brother-in-law staggered backward, then touched the left side of his face before he spoke. "You are a dog. You are nothing."

"I know that."

"You are forever corrupted, and outside the mercy of God. There is no amount of atonement that can redeem you."

"Not true." James dropped to his knees and sobbed. "That's not true. Jesus loves me."

His brother-in-law recoiled from him.

"Go away. Leave me alone." James closed his eyes as he leaned forward to strike the ground with his right fist. "He loves me." Then he struck the ground with his left. "He loves me, I say." He struck the ground again with his right fist, and then with his left and right and left and right and—

He turned away from his dark self, opened his eyes, and encountered the bright eyes of the kind veiled figure, who abandoned him at that canopied establishment after he ate bread and cheese, and drank two cups of milk.

The figure stood before him.

"You again." James was too exhausted by his nightmare to be astonished.

"Yes. This is not reality."

"I had a bad dream."

"And now you will have a good one," the veiled figure pledged.

"Jesus may be fulfilling God's purpose," said James, "but I know I'm not."

"You dare compare yourself to our Lord?"

"I dare speak the truth."

"There's a lot of that going on this night."

"I don't care for your heightened tone." James massaged his temples. "Too much has happened recently."

"You pretend to know what you're talking about."

"I did not pretend to hear Peter swear that he *heard* our Lord speaking to Moses and Elijah when we were with—"

"Peter swore that he *saw* what it appeared to be—"

"Ah. More heightened tone," James interrupted. "Alright. Perhaps Peter saw them with Jesus and thought he heard—wait. You weren't there."

"What else did Peter say?"

James regarded the figure with suspicion as he searched his memory. "Peter said—when our Lord was praying, his face became as bright as the sun and his clothes became dazzling white."

"Peter was dreaming."

"So you say."

"And aren't you dreaming now?"

James was taken aback by this remark. "Well . . . then it . . . it could be that—wait. Was Peter also in a dream when he said that a shining cloud appeared to cover Jesus and Moses and Elijah? And was he in a dream when a voice came from within that cloud?"

"It was *His* voice."

"'*This is my son, whom I am well pleased—listen to him!*' This is what the voice said according to Peter. Was that a dream?" James asked.

"It was *His* voice."

"*His* voice, *His* voice," James repeated, feeling frustrated. "Wait. Our Lord can do anything. Be anything. Be in anything—in our presence or in our dreams. Right?"

The veiled figure did not answer him.

"In and out of time. In and out of visions." James shook his head. "I am so confused."

An involuntary sigh escaped from the veiled figure. "Believe in *Him*. That's all the faith you need. You are saved. You are put right with God."

"Believe." James's expression flattened as he turned away from the figure, then closed his eyes. "What is the meaning of this word, saved? Why hasn't the Holy Spirit provided me with an answer?"

The veiled figure spoke from a distance. "You don't have to understand our Lord's meaning. Believe in the word—*His* word. Have faith in Jesus. Trust in him. That's all you need to know."

James opened his eyes to respond to all this repeated belief and faith, but the veiled figure was gone.

He sat up on his bed mattress and rubbed his eyes in response to the feeble glimmer of dawn that shined through the room's only window, which faced the thoroughfare in front of their dwelling.

His hands hurt.

Then he scanned his surroundings and caught sight of the others who were also awake or had been awakened by—

Chapter 30

Each man had sat up on their bed mattresses.

Each man had been unable to rise further.

The strangeness of their nightmares and dreams had been exhausting.

Their continued silence succumbed to relief, and relief surrendered to the guilt that plagued each of them.

Thomas shuddered. "What happened?"

James released a fragile moan.

Simon took an unsteady breath.

Matthew exhaled. "I had a strange dream."

"For me," said James, "it was no mere dream."

"I had more than a mere dream as well," Matthew confessed. "I had a true nightmare, at first."

James was surprised. "For me as well."

"A nightmare is an understatement," Simon declared.

"I agree," said Thomas.

"But then everything changed suddenly for the better," James continued. "And I . . . I believe I encountered someone who was filled—no—empowered, by the Holy Spirit. Yes." James rubbed his hands together to express his certainty. "My nightmare dissolved into something more important—dissolved into an extraordinary dream."

"Or, perhaps, an extraordinary vision?" Matthew offered.

"A vision," James muttered. "I believe you're right." His amazement grew. "Yes. And for me, that vision began with the visitation of my kind veiled figure."

Matthew's eyes widened. "*My* nightmare ended with the visitation of my immaculate veiled woman."

"Could your woman have been an angel?" James wondered.

"No. But . . . ." Matthew swayed from side to side as he reached for another answer. "But she must have been empowered by the Holy Spirit."

James scratched his face. "Yes. The Holy Spirit."

"My elderly woman was not an angel either," Simon announced.

"In your vision," Matthew verified.

"Yes. That's right. My vision," said Simon. "I also believe she was empowered by the Holy Spirit."

"And my veiled potter," Thomas revealed thoughtfully, "had to be empowered—in my . . . my vision, as well."

"It appears, then, that each one of us had a nightmare," Matthew glanced at Simon for support, "that was followed by a dream, which transformed into an important vision where we encountered the Holy Spirit."

"The Holy Spirit," James repeated.

"Present in our visions," Simon affirmed.

"Sharing wisdom with me." Thomas stated. "Can this be?"

"I believe," Matthew said with careful certainty, "that the Holy Spirit has truly visited each of us through different forms, within different ages—by different men and women . . . ."

"Am I worthy of such a thing happening to me?" Simon asked.

Thomas was overwhelmed. "Are any of us worthy?"

"Have any of us been worthy of our Lord?" This final notion from James brought them all into a humble silence.

Each man sank into an introspection that enhanced their uncertain presence, their unclear spirits, and their unrighteous selves.

With the passage of time, they succumbed to their physical and mental exhaustion and reclined on their bed mattresses.

Introspection gave way to a sleep without dreams or visions, a recovering sleep that was needed by each man.

The continued unfolding of dawn illuminated a room that harbored four injured men.

PART VIII

THE WOMEN AND JESUS

Chapter 31

When the room's trapdoor was pushed open and the back of it hit the floor, all four men were awakened abruptly. As they sat up on their mattresses, the young woman who had led them to this refuge appeared. She was followed by another woman. Both of them were carrying provisions. The young woman brought a large pitcher of milk, the older woman brought bread and dates.

The young woman disciple acknowledged their mid-morning muddle. "I'm sorry we alarmed you."

Matthew scratched his head, then responded. "There is no need for you to apologize for our . . . our—"

"Fear," Simon asserted. "Let's be truthful."

The young woman unfurled her mantle and revealed a beautiful face. "We are all afraid. There is no shame in that." She placed the pitcher of milk on the table and picked up the two empty wine flasks by their necks. Then she went to the trapdoor opening and waited.

The other woman was mature, full-figured, and plain. Her full length tunic was dark-brown, and her coarse mantle was draped around her shoulders like a shawl. It was evident that she was familiar with hard work. In fact, she appeared to have the strength of a midwife.

The mature woman placed two loaves of bread and a bowl of dates on the table. "The bread is fresh." She picked up the empty bowl. "The dates are dried and sweet."

Thomas conveyed his gratitude with a cough.

Matthew bit his lower lip.

James acknowledged her with a slight nod.

Simon spoke. "Thank you." He glanced at the younger woman. "Both of you."

"What are your names?" James inquired. "If I may ask."

"My name is Hadattah," said the mature woman, then indicated her companion. "And her name is Taralah."

The young beauty smiled after hearing her name.

"Whose home is this?" Matthew asked. "We would like to thank him and—"

"That's not important," said Hadattah.

"You are all safe here for now," Taralah added. "That is all you need to know."

"We have been overwhelmed by these recent events," said James.

"That's the truth," Thomas uttered.

Taralah smiled at him. "We understand that."

"I am Thomas."

"I know that," she said.

"We know all your names," Hadattah declared.

"We?" James probed.

"Those of us who were not able, or privileged, to have lived with our Lord Jesus," Taralah qualified.

"We could only be his witness from afar," Hadattah disclosed. "From within the safety of large crowds."

"I see," said James.

"This so-called privilege has been a special kind of burden," Matthew revealed. "Wouldn't you agree, James?"

"Indeed."

"And that's another truth," said Thomas. "I assure you."

Hadattah squinted at him. "That's a strange truth."

Simon cleared his throat. "We won't defend ourselves."

"None of us can," said Matthew.

Hadattah nodded at Taralah before she conveyed her approval. "You're feelings of guilt seem genuine."

The men were relieved by the softening of these two women.

"We have heard that Jesus was washed, anointed, and buried by women disciples," Matthew stated.

"I was one of those women who participated in that," said Hadattah. She noticed their growing humbleness toward her. "Let's have none of that. Please."

"Do either of you," Matthew continued, "know what has happened to our scattered brethren, the other—lost, disciples?"

"No." Taralah pursed her thin lips. "We have neither seen them, nor have we heard anything about them."

Hadattah waved her hands to indicate her helplessness in this matter before she said, "We simply don't know where they are."

"They must be in hiding, like us," said Thomas.

"I hope so," said Taralah. "Because truthfully, I was simply fortunate to discover you—all of you. Because you were all behaving like outcasts and vagrants and—wait." She pointed at Thomas. "You were behaving like a fugitive from, yes—*you* . . . and you were the fugitives of Gethsemane." She pointed at another man with each following *you* and you. "All the women on the mound knew that *you* and you were our Lord's disciples. We knew that all of *you* and you here had been spending the recent nights at Gethsemane. We saw that *you* and you were obviously out of place among us—the women of Golgotha. And I realized that the next squad of Legionnaires that marched across the hill were going to stop and arrest all of you. Yes. It was fortunate that I found you upon my return to Golgotha. And it was fortunate that I found the courage to offer all of you my help."

"Yes, fortunate," Matthew agreed. "Truly fortunate because of *your* courage."

"A small courage," Taralah qualified. "Let us hope that your brethren disciples have been fortunate as well."

"Because the truth is," Hadattah added, "this city, and the surrounding countryside, is thick with Legionnaires and Temple Guards. They are arresting any man who seems out of place, or who acts suspiciously. Any man. You have good reason to be afraid."

"Thank you for that," said Matthew. "Since our Lord's arrest, we have not been ourselves or . . . or . . . ."

"Ourselves," James remarked. "I fear that, perhaps, this is who we really *are* without our Lord. Fearful men. Trembling men. Defeated men."

Taralah responded to him with sympathy. "That's *very* honest."

"Who you really *are* . . . ." Hadattah leveled her gaze at James. "I think you are too unforgiving of yourself." Then she regarded each man in turn before she said, "All of you."

"That's very kind of you," said Matthew. "I'm not sure we deserve that."

"But we'll take it!" Simon filled the small room with his gratitude.

Hadattah was delighted by his generous response. "I am surprised by the strong effect that my little kindness has had on you."

"Not so little coming from . . . from a godly woman, who took part in washing and anointing our Lord."

Hadattah was warmed by Simon's acknowledgment. "There was no need for you to say that."

Her sincere humbleness brought a genuine smile upon Simon's face, and brought a measure of joy to the others.

"We have not been able to feel at ease for quite some time," said James. "Thank you for this, Hadattah—and you, Taralah." He folded his arms across his chest to indicate that he also had something serious to add. "But what now? What can we do? What must we do?"

"Pray." The simplicity and the truth of Hadattah's answer startled James and the other men in the room.

"My God!" said Simon.

"Yes," Matthew whispered.

"Of course," Thomas agreed.

James was the first of them to kneel with the women.
Matthew was next.

James waited for Simon and Thomas to join them
before he pressed the palms of his hands together. "Let us
pray."

And they prayed. Without understanding. They prayed.
Without expectation. And they prayed.

Without knowing.

Chapter 32

Soon after the women left the room, the men ended their spiritual efforts due to aching injuries, nagging guilt, and sinking depression. And after fortifying their worn out bodies with the food and the milk that the women had brought them, they succumbed to their debilitating exhaustion, which led them back into another slumber.

When they rose from their mattresses again, they openly and collectively took care of their physical needs in the covered pots that were set against the wall near the trapdoor. Except for Matthew, this was ordinary behavior for fishermen, who freely took care of such needs when they were working offshore on-board their boats, at any hour—in direct contrast to the newly developed private behavior of each man toward his physical needs, which occurred during the still hours of these recent hidden days and nights.

They also tended to their wounds by using the water that was available in the large copper vessel, which stood tall against the wall opposite the trapdoor entrance.

A stack of large washbowls and towels were set along one side of the copper vessel to accommodate their personal hygiene. And there were several buckets stacked against the other side of the vessel to provide the means to dispose of the dirty water from the washbowls. A long-handled ladle rested against the front of the copper vessel.

Not long after they completed their personal and medical needs, the women brought them more food—a little offering of milk and bread and honey. Hadattah also brought a plain pair of sandals, which she placed at the foot of Matthew's mattress. And when she noticed that he was deeply moved by her thoughtfulness, she prevented his attempt to verbally thank her with a dismissive back-handed wave.

In fact, there were no expressions of gratitude permitted for the services that Hadattah, or Taralah, were providing: the room clean up and the dining table reset; the content disposal of both the covered pots and the filled buckets.

There were no verbal exchanges.

After the women were gone, Matthew broke the uncomfortable silence among them. "These women always manage to know what to do, and to know when to remain silent."

"They also seem to know our Lord," said James.

"That's true," Matthew agreed. "Our women do seem to listen to him with more understanding. Yes. Yes. They do. And, I must confess that I often observed their understanding when Jesus spoke to the countryside crowds."

"That's right," said James. "They did listen with great interest."

"I listened!" Thomas interjected.

"And you often did not comprehend," James countered. "Like me."

"Thomas, look at it this way," said Matthew. "You heard our Lord speak about the same things many times and, yet, here you are, and—"

"Here *we* are," James inserted. "And, here *they* are—look at them. These women seem to know more about our Lord than we do—even with having less exposure to him." He addressed Matthew. "How is that possible?"

"Our women followed him as devotedly as we did through the years," Matthew reasoned—then solemnly, "But, yes, it is true—most of them heard him from a distance within the crowds."

"But many of them also heard the same stories numerous times," said Simon, in Thomas's defense.

"That is true, as well," said Matthew. "But, somehow, they have often discovered something new and deeper in the words that our Lord repeated."

"How is that possible?" Simon conceded.

Matthew hesitated. "I don't know."

"And none of them had to be *called* either," James disclosed.

"None?" Thomas was skeptical. "Are you sure about that?"

"Name me one."

Thomas stammered while he searched his memory.

"You can't," said Matthew. "But they were always, somehow, present."

Thomas acknowledge Matthew, then James. "How could I have missed that?"

"I must join my ignorance with yours," Simon remarked, as he cast his sheepish expression at Thomas. "This has never occurred to me either."

Thomas's bewilderment deepened. "Now that I'm aware of this, it occurs to *me* that our women also rarely questioned our Lord."

James was startled by this insight. "I believe—I believe you're right."

"They were simply present." Thomas's amazement increased with James's validation. "They served him without question."

"And I must admit," said James, "it was truly rare to see a woman, or a girl, upset in his presence."

"And also," Matthew added with a growing admiration, "I can't remember an incident when a woman didn't have faith in him." He pursed his lips. "It seems to be a natural force within them to believe—in him. I don't understand that."

"Wait," said Simon. "I think I remember something. Hold on." He took a moment to clarify his recollection. "While we were weaving our way southward through Judea to where we are now, I remember a woman chiding her sister, who was sitting at the feet of our Lord listening to him teach." He snapped his fingers. "That's right. And I think *that* chiding was a matter concerning faith. If I have remembered this correctly, she seemed to be trying to gain a special favor from our Lord in her own way."

"I'm not so sure about *that*," Matthew differed. "It seems to me, if I have remembered correctly, the woman that you're speaking of simply wanted her sister to help prepare their home, and help cook the evening meal—for him. Our Lord's visits were always unannounced. You know that." He leveled his gaze at Simon. "I'm sorry. I disagree. I remember I felt sympathy for that woman, who was caught up in her preparations for him—and for us. You know how Jesus was."

"Yes, yes," Simon agreed. "But I also know this: our Lord wanted that woman to gain favor in *His* way."

"Ah." Matthew considered Simon's statement. "He wanted her to stop and sit at his feet, and listen—then and there. I see."

"They *are* human," said Thomas. "They have their faults."

"That's true," James intruded. "But how often did that happen to us?"

Thomas grinned timidly. "You mean, how often did I not stop what I was doing on his behalf of . . . of . . . ."

"There you are." James produced a broken smile. "You've caught the idea." And with increased intensity, he added, "We had three years on the road with him to get this right."

"I listened," Thomas insisted. "I listened."

"So did I." Then Simon conceded. "But now, I've come to realize that I did not stop to listen to our Lord often enough. And, therefore, I did not often hear him deeply—like most women surely did, except for the one I mentioned here."

"But there's no triumph there," said Matthew, "by drawing some comfort in thinking that you may have observed that one of our women didn't always choose the right thing to do when it came to listening to our Lord. There's no triumph because I don't believe she was doing anything wrong in wanting to set a proper table for us— and our Lord. Besides, what's wrong with her being able to listen to our Lord while she tended to his needs? Women can do that."

"Alright, alright." Simon surrendered. "I'm wrong. I must confess, I didn't feel satisfied when I revealed my recollection about her."

"I believe I heard *that* in the tone of your voice from the very beginning of your challenge," said Matthew.

"You're right. Damn you." Simon smiled. "It's true. I *was* unsure of my argument from the beginning."

"Why?"

Simon smirked. "Because, I do feel—as I now know you do—that our women often understood our Lord more deeply than us. Normally, I would feel resentful, but somehow I do not." He leveled his gaze at Matthew. "And almost more importantly, I feel that their believing thoughts of him can't be taken away from them."

"Is that what has happened to us since our Lord's arrest?" James wondered. "Have our believing thoughts of him been taken away?"

"Nonsense!"

"*That*, coming from you, Thomas?" James was amazed. "Well, I have to be honest and confess that my belief has been in question recently."

"Don't say that," Thomas warned. "You've been told the consequences of that. Damn. This is what happens when men speak of women."

"Then I will have to think it," James declared.

"Stop this," Matthew demanded. "Both of you. All of you. All of us."

Matthew shook so intensely with self-recrimination that the others were compelled to remain quiet, and listen attentively to him.

"Look at us. Where would we be now without these fine women disciples of our Lord, who seem superior to us in their faith. Look at them. Then look at us." He pressed his hands against his chest to express humility. "We are doomed despite their love. And we are doomed by thinking we have lost our believing thoughts about our Lord, Jesus. Let us stop this, here and now. Here and now."

Chapter 33

They had grown restless in this place of hiding. Another day had passed since their Lord's arrest, crucifixion, and death.

They were on the edge of having an argument when Hadattah pushed open the trapdoor, prevented the back of it from slamming against the floor, and called out to them. "Supper will be brought up to you shortly. Is it safe to enter?"

James snickered with embarrassment. "Of course. Please join us. You're just in time."

She climbed over the top of the ladder, then stepped into the room. She turned to them after she shut the trapdoor. "For what?"

"To prevent us from having an argument," said James.

"I thought I heard—" She set her arms akimbo. "About what?"

"Our faith."

She was perplexed. "What about faith?"

"It seems to have been misplaced," said James.

"How can that be?" She relaxed her stance, glanced at each man, then raised her right hand toward James for emphasis. "You have been his disciple. Didn't you understand the meaning of the stories that our Lord shared with you?"

"Always never," James admitted.

"Be serious," she said.

"I'm almost serious," James insisted. "Believe me. I always struggled to understand the meaning behind what he taught me."

"He always spoke the truth," she said.

"You're right," Matthew intervened, in defense of James. "However, let's say, when he spoke of divorce—I didn't know if it was truly divorce that he was speaking about, or something else. There was always an underlying meaning, concerning the truth, that was different from the subject that he was speaking about."

"Which always mystified me," said James.

"Always," Thomas insisted, in support of James.

"And I must admit," Simon interjected, "his teachings concerning wealth and prosperity always confounded me."

"Yes," Thomas added. "The rich and the poor. The master and the servant. The ruler and the slave. Where in these opposites do I fit into, I wonder? Who am I?"

"A believer—in *Him*," said Hadattah.

"Yes. Yes. Of course." James exhaled resignation. "I always fell under his influence when I was near him. But the trick is, how do I remain within his influence when he is not present?"

"He said he would always be present," said Hadattah.

"Then where is he?" Simon implored.

"I'm not sure," she confessed. "But I can almost hear him say: *you of little faith*."

"See?" Thomas grumbled. "We're hopeless."

"And that's the truth," Simon emphasized.

"Please," Matthew implored. "Take us away from ourselves, Hadattah. Please. Share with us what you know about our Lord's death."

"Were you truly there during his crucifixion?" James inquired.

She addressed him with sincere humility. "Yes."

"Speak to us," James pleaded. "Share with us what you witnessed—if you can."

Hadattah seriously considered his request, which required her to reach into her sorrowful recollection about what she had witnessed. "'*Forgive them, Father! They do not know what they are doing*.'" Her plain and ruddy face softened after she shared that moment of remembrance. "Do you see? Do you understand what he said? To the bitter end, he spoke of forgiveness." She paused momentarily to hold back her tears. "Our Lord never, never wavered about love."

"Share more with us, please, this expression of love, while Jesus was dying on the cross—if you can," James implored.

With the inhale of an intentional breath, it seemed as if she was preparing to reproduce the tone of Jesus' agonized voice. "'*Woman, here is your son*,' our Lord said."

"I don't understand that," said James.

"To his Mother," Hadattah explained. "He was speaking to his Mother."

"Speaking to her about what?" Thomas asked.

"'*Here is your son*,' our Lord said to *her*—about *John*. He stood near her, and remained speechless." Hadattah composed herself before she spoke. There was a tone of certainty in her voice. "And, *I believe* that our Lord meant that John represented all sons, all daughters, all disciples— all who believed in *Him*. Our Lord's mother is to be *our* mother."

"That is a woman's explanation," Thomas claimed.

"Hold your tongue," Simon countered. "Show some respect for this lady."

Thomas assented by turning his palms outward from where they were at his side.

Simon directed a gentle gaze at Hadattah. "Go on. Please."

"And then," Hadattah paused once again before she said, "Our Lord simply said to John, '*Here is your Mother.*'"

"Ah. Now I see," said James.

"So, one of us *was truly there*, after all," Matthew affirmed.

"But while hiding," Thomas clarified. "Among women."

"Damn your eyes." Simon glared at Thomas to emphasis his reproach. "Like *us*."

"But more openly present, it seems," Matthew assured, furthering John's defense.

"Yes, that's right," James stated. "More openly than ourselves."

"So it seems." Simon further hardened his gaze at Thomas. "And *among* women."

"Among women," Matthew repeated. "Yes.

"And so—she is to be our Mother?" was Thomas's grudging response to Hadattah. "I'm sorry. I don't understand."

James admonished him. "You mean, you won't."

She sought Simon's assistance. "I believe you would be better equipped to explain this further to him than I would."

"But there you are," said Simon. "I don't know how. Because I'm not clear in my own understanding as well."

"He's telling you the truth," James insisted, in support of Simon's honesty—and with respect for her. "Sadly, we don't seem to know anything. We haven't been able to . . . to . . . ."

"Well," she intruded, to rescue James from his inability to express himself further. "He often *did* speak in a heightened manner."

"Yes. And so indirectly," said James. "He was often so indirect. I don't know why."

"You. Or you." She smiled at Simon. "Yes. You would know better about that than me, a mere follower from the distance."

Simon folded his arms across his large chest and returned her smile. "Not so distant anymore, as far as I'm concerned."

"He's right," said James. "You were there *with him* when he was dying on the cross. We weren't." He glanced at Simon. "We are in the distance now, I think."

She softened again with another recollection. "'*I am thirsty,*' our Lord said."

"*That* sounds direct to me," said Thomas.

Hadattah ignored Thomas's interruption. "'*It is finished,*' he said. Then he died." She composed herself. "What more do you want to know?"

"This . . . this remains confusing to me," Simon confessed. "In life, he spoke indirectly. In death's final moment, he spoke directly. How am I to understand that?"

"Don't understand," said Hadattah.

"*That's* no answer," Thomas admonished.

Simon glowered at him.

"Wait," said Matthew. "I believe Simon might have stumbled upon something close to indicating an answer. I think."

"He thinks, he says. He thinks," Thomas jeered.

"Perhaps in his sudden directness," Matthew persisted, "Jesus was showing us *all* the way to death. What do you think, Hadattah? You were there."

"'*It is finished,*'" she repeated with an increase of emotion, then leveled a steady gaze at Matthew. "Direct. Indirect. This does not matter." She reached deeply within herself in order to explain what she had witnessed. "When I stood before him with my sisters, I suddenly understood that my Lord Jesus was suffering the wrath of God while dying on the cross for my sins—and for the sins of the world. Imagine that. Imagine what that amount of suffering must have been. The wrath of God!" She studied their bedazzled expressions. She realized how deeply they were listening to her. "No wonder our Lord Jesus cried during his long suffering on that cross, "'*My God, my God, why did you abandon me?*'" She leveled a gentle gaze at them. "From my heart, I believe he meant: why is this taking so long?" There was certainty in the tone of her voice. "No one else could have suffered the wrath of God —for all the sins of the world." She smiled. "What a gift it was to hear this— then and there. This glimpse into his suffering was a gift from him—to me." She inhaled thoughtfully, then exhaled. "And now, here I am, sharing what I know to you, because of what I have witnessed."

One by one, each man knelt before her, not in worship, but with respect.

Had Hadattah been filled by the Holy Spirit? Had she been possessed by the Holy Spirit?

They did not know. And yet, somehow, they did know, without consulting each other, that it seemed as if the Holy Spirit must have been present, in her, through her— yes, through this humble woman standing before them.

"We are strangers and refugees in this world," James whispered.

"And we thank you," said Matthew, "for what you have shared."

Simon, and Thomas, reacted with grateful nods because they were filled with the kind of gratitude that could not be expressed in words.

Before Hadattah could respond to all this sincere gratitude, the trapdoor was thrown open, which caused a large crash when the back of it hit the floor. The cracking sound of wood hitting wood brought everyone back to an ordinary present.

Taralah announced that supper was forthcoming as she ascended the ladder.

The men ate lightly, drank heavily, and spoke little. Then they slept hard into the third night after their Lord's arrest.

PART IX

THE ESCAPE

Chapter 34

They were awakened the following morning by the aggressive sound of Roman Legionnaires marching by their limestone hideaway. With a collective inhale of self-control, they listened to this nearby danger.

They sat up on their mattresses and waited.

Simon stood up, crept to the small window that over-looked the thoroughfare below, and examined the situation outside.

"What is it?" asked Thomas.

"Shh," was Simon's initial response before he whispered, "Two squads. Marching in strict formation toward each other."

"What else?"

"Shh. Wait."

James covered his mouth with his right hand to prevent a nervous cough from escaping.

Matthew clenched his hands together.

"Legionnaires seem to be everywhere," Simon whispered.

Cruel laughter erupted from both formations in response to the hails between their squad leaders.

"What was that?" Thomas asked.

"Roman humor while marching by each other," said Simon. "Whatever that is—wait a moment. Shh."

"What?"

Simon demanded silence from Thomas by raising his left hand.

Matthew bit his lower lip and shared his disquieted expression with James.

Simon eased away from the window and approached Thomas. "They're gone."

"I don't understand this heavy presence," said Thomas. "Our Lord's crucifixion would have been an ordinary execution, according to Rome."

"Maybe it's not about the execution," Matthew offered.

"Be sensible," said James. "What other reason could there be for so many Legionnaires moving through the lower city? Rome doesn't care about this poverty-stricken area."

Simon exhaled vexation. "They could be looking for us."

"We're not that important," said Matthew.

Thomas slapped his thigh. "We need to get out of here."

"And go where?" James asked.

"Shh," Simon cautioned. "What's that I hear?"

The trapdoor squeaked as it was pushed open. Hadattah appeared while carefully setting the back of the door onto the floor without dropping it. She waved at them to remain calm as she continued ascending the ladder. When she entered the room, Taralah emerged at the top of the ladder. After she stepped into the room, a man appeared at the trapdoor entrance.

The tension in the room intensified as the man entered the room.

Simon started to challenge the man, but Taralah pressed her right index finger against her lips and insisted that he remain quiet. More danger could be heard approaching them.

Everyone listened to another squad of Legionnaires passing by. They waited patiently until the sound of the squad faded into the distance.

As soon as Taralah removed her finger from her mouth, Hadattah whispered to Simon, "This man will escort you to safety."

Simon addressed the man. "I don't know you."

"I am a follower of our Lord, Jesus."

All four men stirred uneasily. They regarded him with suspicion.

James glanced at Matthew, then at Thomas. "*We* don't know you."

The man shifted his weight onto his right leg. "There are many of us that you don't know. But *we* know you." He scrutinized them. "All of you."

"Who are *we*?" Simon challenged.

"We are those who have stood in the crowds and have listened to our Lord's teachings from a distance."

Matthew's tension softened. "Ah. Yes. Of course." He glanced at Hadattah, then at Taralah. "We've been told about this. Please forgive us. We are constantly not ourselves lately."

The man pulled off his round cap to convey his understanding, and respect. "I'm Joiada, son of Ezra."

He was bald headed, short in stature, and overweight. His knee-length tunic, which was tied at the waist with a thick leather belt, exposed his hairy legs—the tunic's short sleeves also exposed his hairy forearms. A thick brown beard caressed his gentle smile and accentuated his bright eyes. Two fingers of his left hand were missing.

"And I'm Matthew."

"I know." Joiada acknowledged each man after he replaced his cap upon his bald head. "I know all your names."

Thomas drew Joiada's attention by issuing a cough. "It seems like everybody knows who we are now that our Lord is no longer with us."

Joiada hesitated. "I'm not sure I understand what you are implying." Joiada shrugged. "I am here to help you."

Matthew grabbed Thomas by the upper left arm. "Forgive his rudeness, and his continued doubts. It has always been a fault of his."

Thomas pulled his arm free. "Of ours, you mean."

"Shh. All of you." Simon hurried to the window and peeked outside.

"What is it?" Matthew whispered.

Simon dismissed him with a backhanded wave.

Everyone remained quiet and still while Simon investigated the noise that he thought he heard outside.

Simon relaxed. "It's nothing." He moved away from the window, then turned to Joiada before he whispered, "Sorry. Matthew is right. We continue not to be ourselves yet."

"He speaks for all of us," said James.

Joiada waved both of his hands at them in sympathy. "Enough of that. Please. No more apologies. Please. I'm a mere coppersmith and . . . and a believer in our Lord Jesus—like you." He sensed their expanding relief. "And as Hadattah has already indicated, I am here to take you to a safer place. But we must wait until nightfall."

"What is happening out there?" James inquired. "Why are there so many Legionnaires on patrol? Who are they looking for? Surely, not us."

"That's right." Thomas raised both of his hands to emphasize his concern. "We are not that important." He peered at Simon for support. "Or are we?"

Joiada licked his dry lips, then glanced at both women before he answered. "Our Lord's tomb—it was found empty this morning."

Matthew was astounded. "Empty?"

"Yes."

"Are you . . . you *sure* about that?" Thomas sputtered.

"Absolutely sure," Joiada insisted.

"So." Thomas hesitated. "These . . . these Legionnaires must be looking for . . . for our Lord?"

"I believe they are looking for those who stole his body," said Joiada.

"Did you witness this empty tomb yourself?" Thomas importuned.

"No." Joiada clasped his hands together. "But these women have."

Thomas addressed Taralah. "Did you?"

She took a single step toward him. "Mary of Magdala, our sister, was the first person to discover the empty tomb."

James was filled with wonder. "Mary."

"And it was there," Hadattah added, "that an angel spoke to her and to—"

"An angel?" Simon interrupted.

Matthew approached her. "How do you know for sure that it was an angel?"

"Never mind that," said Hadattah. "Listen to me. There is more news." She continued speaking after she was certain that they would remain silent. "Mary encountered this angel, who was wearing a white robe. He was standing inside our Lord's empty tomb. He told her that Jesus of Nazareth had been raised. And then he told her to inform his disciples about this."

"And how was this news brought to you?" James asked.

"Through Mary—and through the other women who had accompanied her to the tomb."

"I see," said James.

Hadattah placed her right palm above her breasts. "There's one more thing."

James's eyes widened. "Yes?"

"Mary was told by the angel to take a message to his disciples, which I am now sharing with you."

"Go on, please."

Hadattah inhaled as she reached into her memory. "The angel said: '*He is going to Galilee ahead of you; there you will see him, just as he told you.*'"

"Are you sure about this?" Matthew asked.

"Of course. At first, Mary and the others were afraid to say anything to the men."

Matthew was surprised. "Afraid?"

"But they overcame that fear by sharing this news to other women." She caught Matthew's startled expression. "Why are you so surprised about that?"

Neither Matthew nor the other men could respond to her question.

"No matter," she continued. "I have brought you the message. And now, now you know that he has risen."

Matthew pressed his clasped hands against his chin before sharing his thoughts with her. "Our Lord Jesus told us that he was going to rise from the dead many times. And that death would be defeated for all time—through him."

Hadattah crossed her arms beneath her breasts. "Our Lord's Mother was also told by this angel that Jesus had been raised—just as he said."

"Mother of God," said James. "There it is. This could all be truly true."

Taralah glanced at Hadattah. "We know it's true. Our Lord has risen." And with this stunning statement of finality, she extended her right hand to Hadattah, who took it with her left.

Together, the women approached the trapdoor, which had been left open.

"Where are you going?" Thomas implored.

Hadattah released Taralah's hand and stepped onto the ladder.

"Where are you going?" Thomas repeated.

Taralah stepped onto the ladder after Hadattah was halfway into her descent.

"Take us with you," James pleaded.

As Taralah descended the ladder, she simply stated, "Lord Jesus' tomb was found empty." Then she disappeared underneath the trapdoor, which she closed above her.

James turned to Joiada. "Where are they going?"

"Never mind them. You need to go where I take you tonight," said Joiada. "It is where the others are hiding."

All four disciples drew a little closer to Joiada.

"You mean you know where Peter and the others are?" Matthew inquired.

"Yes. They are safe—and they are as frightened as you are."

"Do they know what happened to Our Lord on Golgotha?" Thomas asked.

"Of course."

"And what about this morning?" James demanded. "Do they know what has happened this morning?"

"That, I do not know," said Joiada.

Simon was visibly irritated. "How come these women did not inform us about where the others were after all this time being here?"

"They did not know anything about your brethren disciples until I arrived here this morning."

Simon was suddenly suspicious. "How did *you* find out about us being here?"

"That's right," Thomas insisted. "How did you know we were here?"

"Any kind of questionable behavior like the arrival of strangers, who were escorted by a young woman into a district like this, would—"

"Then . . . then we were noticed," Thomas interjected.

"Of course you were. The arrival of all outsiders are always noticed. And then, you were seen not leaving."

"Ah. Yes," said Simon. "That would be suspicious indeed."

"And word spreads easily," Joiada explained. "Especially in this lower city. That's why you need to leave this place tonight. It's no longer safe to stay here. I will lead you to your new destination."

"Tonight." Thomas qualified.

"It will be less dangerous then."

"Where will you take us?" Simon asked.

"To where your brethren disciples are safely hidden," he repeated.

"In the countryside?" James pressed.

"Yes, yes." Joiada yielded. "They are staying with a generous sheepherder—another follower of Jesus. They're hidden in his sheepfold stable outside a small village. It is quite humble, but you will be comfortable and secure there."

"Is it far from here?" James persisted.

"Some distance. But not terribly far from the city's wall." Joiada raised his hands for emphasis. "You'll see."

Matthew was careful to ask. "Are the others alright?"

"Yes. And they'll be glad to see you, I'm sure."

"Are they all there?" Matthew probed.

"All but one."

Matthew glanced furtively at James, then at the others. Their eyes narrowed. Their lips tightened.

Joiada noticed their strange response to this piece of news. He cleared his throat. "Did I say something wrong?"

"No," said Matthew. "You said nothing wrong."

Well." Joiada hesitated. "You will certainly find out which one of you is missing after I take you to them."

"If we get there," said Thomas.

"Remain steady today." Then Joiada acknowledged each of them before he said, "I *will* get you there."

All this extraordinary news continued to astound Matthew. "He has risen—for all time. He has risen."

"For all time." Thomas was mystified. "Do you really think so?"

"Of course he has," James responded with increasing hope and wonder. "Jesus said he would—many times. He said that—"

"It will be written," Matthew fully recalled. "'*God will kill the shepherd and the sheep will all be scattered. But after I am raised to life, I will go to Galilee ahead of you.*' That's what our Lord said. Remember?"

James acknowledged Matthew, then peered at Simon, who was simply unable to enhance what Matthew said.

"Then we must go to Galilee." Thomas observed that everyone else was deeply involved in some kind of a reverie—of their own making. "Alright then—*He* has risen."

James was transfixed by his thoughts. "Then we will go to Galilee."

"Yes," Matthew added. "As soon as it is safe enough for us to reach the countryside. Until then, it is lower Jerusalem that will save us from Rome. Jerusalem will continue to hide us today and keep us safe until . . . until—"

"We see our Lord again," James announced from within the rapture that continued to infect him. "For he has risen. As he said he would."

"Hold on you two—wait—all of you," Simon commanded. "We must meet Peter and the others first. Remember?" Simon waited for everyone to shake themselves free of their awe, before he leveled a steady gaze at Joiada. "This man will lead us to another safety. And then—"

"We will know more about what to do, and where to go, once we are all together again," said Thomas.

"Together again," Matthew repeated. "That sounds right."

"Yes," said James. "Together."

Simon folded the fingers of his right hand over the back of his left hand. "All *will* be right."

Chapter 35

Escape and evasion while traveling through the dark thoroughfares and passing by the ominous alleyways and scurrying along the mean byroads of Jerusalem, established their disquieted behavior.

Their recently attained news, however, established their present destination—a sheepfold stable outside of the city where their fellow disciples were in hiding.

They hurried through Jerusalem's dangerous labyrinth as if they were being chased by a monstrous beast.

"Slow down," Joiada implored. "We are drawing too much attention to ourselves."

An old man with a twisted body hobbled across their path. They heard scraps of the old man's maniacal chatter.

"Look there. Do you see that?" Joiada whispered.

They slowed down to a nervous walk.

"That was a harmless madman," said Thomas.

"Madman. Maybe. Or maybe not," Joiada cautioned. "My intention is not to lead you into captivity."

Joiada entered an open courtyard of a sprawling multi-level structure and waited for the others to join him.

"Why are we stopping here?" Simon asked.

Joiada stood at the entrance of the courtyard and surveyed the outer darkness. "To see if we have attracted any serious danger."

James leaned against a wall. "How would you know that? There have been homeless men, women, and children camped on almost every road-crossing, under all outside stairways, and against most doorways that we have traveled passed. Surely they have noticed our presence."

"That kind of passive notice that you are referring to means nothing," said Joiada. "But if it's perceived that there is flight toward a destination that could lead to some kind of reward, a reward that could improve their condition while living in this corrupt and dirty city, well then, *that's* when being noticed arouses serious attention, and becomes dangerous."

"Some kind of reward?" James pressed.

"Yes. A reward that would be violently taken—whatever they hope that reward might be."

"They will be disappointed," said Thomas.

Joiada ignored his remark.

James heeded Joiada's coarse references to Jerusalem. "What kind of city is this?"

"A city. Like any other." Joiada inhaled a deep breath for effect, then exhaled as he directed his attention outside the courtyard once again. "Look. Out there, as in most cities—but especially this city . . . ." He made a show of scrutinizing the vicinity beyond the courtyard's entrance. "Believe me, there are eyes behind every window and ears against every wall—including within this courtyard. There are traitors everywhere. We are being seen and heard and, maybe . . . maybe we are being measured for an assault by savage cutthroats, right now."

"He's right," said Simon.

Matthew came alongside Joiada and peered into his cynical darkness. "A city like any other. Yes."

"Believe me," Joiada insisted. "There is a desperation that travels without footsteps. And that kind of desperation is very dangerous."

Matthew took a calming breath. "I know."

"I'm convinced." James squatted to calm his nerves.

"So—what must we do?" Matthew asked.

"Appear casual," Joiada instructed.

"Casual." Matthew repeated, before he addressed the others. "Casual."

Thomas raised his hands toward the sky. "Alright." He lowered his hands to his side. "Casual. See?"

"Look at us." Simon peered at James, then at Matthew. "Instructions are needed here for survival. Ridiculous. God help us all."

A genuine calm spread slowly among them, which reassured Joiada. "Good. Now let us proceed to the nearest gate. Hopefully, there will be fewer Legionnaires in the countryside."

"What if that is not so?" James asked.

"Then we will have to rely on this present darkness to protect us."

"That is not giving me comfort," said James.

Joiada ignored him. "Is everybody ready?"

"Yes, yes," Simon answered. "Let's go."

They stepped out of the courtyard and proceeded more cautiously across the city.

As soon as they saw the glow of the gatekeeper's lantern, Joiada had them stay where they were while he approached the gate to find out if it was safe for them to pass through the needle's eye. All but Simon fretted as they waited.

When Joiada returned, he beckoned them to hurry. "Come, come. The gatekeeper appears to be sound. And more importantly, there are no Roman sentries posted nearby.

Once through the needle's eye, they advanced successfully into the countryside.

Chapter 36

Although the escape across Jerusalem in an effort to reach their destination succeeded without incident, the journey had been difficult. But when they entered the countryside, the dark hours of the night were so deep that travel became slower and more difficult. In fact, because of the inky darkness they encountered, each man walked like a blind man without the aid of a stick to probe the way ahead.

After traveling a reasonable distance away from the city, Joiada's decision to stop and wait for the first light of dawn was welcomed by everybody. "It is too thick a night to continue traveling. I am sightless."

The weary disciples were glad to agree, and were glad to sit and rest within the security of an acceptable thicket that they had managed to stumble upon.

The deceptive safety of their present place of hiding, along with the passage of time, seduced them into easing their vigilance and unfurling their emotional strain.

James was the first to unravel some of his tension by looking up into the thick and murky night and raising his right hand toward the one celestial body that had managed to pierce through the firmament's hard gloom. "Look. Up there. Do you see? Up there. I wonder. Is that the Day Star that I see peeking through?"

Thomas grumbled as he squirmed from where he sat in an effort to get comfortable. "Stop seeking out the new day. It will come when it comes."

James snickered.

"Leave James alone," said Matthew.

"I'll be glad when we join the others," Thomas announced.

James chuckled mischievously, then nudged Joiada with his elbow. "What happens to the central fire when it disappears—when it becomes hidden by the ground beneath our feet?"

"I have also wondered about that." Joiada was glad to be included into the intimate circle of these true disciples. "And what happens to the fixed heavenly bodies above, as well as the numerous moving celestial wonders, which travel across the sky?"

Thomas admonished him. "God's celestial wonders are not to be understood."

James continued to annoy Thomas with his persistent playfulness. "Why not?"

Thomas surveyed the firmament in an effort to devise another answer to James's challenge. But unenlightened silence was his response.

"But wait. Listen." James lost the lightness in his voice. "What's happening? Up there. Listen. In the distance. Is that a storm brewing?"

Thomas scoffed at him.

Distant thunder rolled toward them, which indicated the approach of bad weather.

Simon peered at the sky. "Hold on there, Thomas. Listen to that. James is right."

"What's happening up there?" Matthew wondered.

"I've never experienced such frequent extremes," said Joiada. "These last few days have been alarming."

It began to rain.

James became more concerned by the celestial activity above than by the change in the weather. "The firmament itself seems to be in turmoil. I wonder if that turmoil could be the cause of these frequent and extreme weather changes. I wonder—wait. Could that turmoil above be a sign of . . . of—could the world be coming to an end?"

"It feels like rain to me," said Thomas.

"These celestial signs above could also be announcing that the world is coming to another beginning," said Matthew.

"To another . . . .Beginning of what?" Simon asked.

"Of our Lord's new presence?" Matthew offered. "Because he has risen?"

"That is," Thomas warned, "if he has truly risen."

"Your absolute need to doubt has changed your mind already?" James sighed to express his exasperation. "How can you persist in your . . . your uncertainty—in your constantly surfacing doubts after all that has happened? And, after all you have been told."

"Yes," said Matthew. "Our Thomas can persist. Even though it must be true. Isn't it? He has risen. Right? I *know* it."

"And that *knowing*," Simon offered, in an effort blunt the edge of Matthew's own mild uncertainty, "is far more important than knowing where the heavenly bodies go during the day or in what direction they go during the night. Right, James?"

"Wait there, you," Thomas contended. "All of you are . . . are objecting too mightily about my doubt."

"Maybe. But Simon, and Matthew, are right." James leaned toward Simon before he said, "And I suppose, and I hope, that this *knowing* includes my continued struggle toward my *faith* that he has risen, as well as my continued struggle toward my faith in *Him*."

Simon leaned toward James before he shared his own concern. "Continued. Yes. I am determined to hope so as well."

James stretched out his arms with his palms turned upward. "Rain." Then he pulled his upper mantle over his head.

"Enough of this," said Thomas. "I think we should proceed to our destination."

"Not so fast," said Joiada. "Not in this weather. And not within this kind of darkness."

"Why not?"

"Bad visibility," Simon grumbled. "You're a fool, Thomas. Don't you realize that we continue to be blind? We are unable to see. Look. In every direction. Look.

There's nowhere that can be seen. And look, Thomas, neither you nor I can see the other's face."

"And let's not forget," Matthew added, "There's no knowing who we might encounter out there in that thick darkness and strange weather. Right, Joiada?"

"That's true. This is no ordinary countryside that surrounds Jerusalem. Very dangerous. Rome's presence is the least of it."

"I agree with that," said Simon.

Thomas grunted in response.

When the rains increased, they huddled close together to seek warmth against the weather.

They had to remain within the relative safety of the sparse thicket; they had to submit to the discomforts of the rising storm.

Chapter 37

The night's ruthlessness was relentless.

Heavy rain fell with claps of thunder.

Streaks of lightening sliced through a disturbed firmament.

Severe winds blew through their sparse thicket.

Endless discomfort tormented all those sitting in the huddle.

James protected his eyes from the rain with his right hand as he gazed into the darkness. "Where do the birds go with the thunder?"

"Here we go again," Thomas complained.

The others chuckled.

The rain intensified.

"Where does daylight go when it becomes night?" Matthew added, to further irritate Thomas.

James shifted his weight onto the left side of his buttocks. "Now there's a question for you."

Thomas was almost amused. "Don't listen to those two, Joiada. They're teasing me. They are both dreamers." He crossed his arms tightly over his chest.

"Shh. Hold it. All of you," Simon whispered, as he shifted onto his knees. "I think I see something moving. Wait. Something *is* moving out there."

"What? Where?" Thomas asked.

"Over there. Hold still," Simon cautioned. "Bandit-scavengers, I think."

Matthew crawled alongside Simon to see for himself. "How do you know that? I can't see anything."

"Look hard," Simon whispered. "Over there. Black ghosts. They're walking without fear. Without care."

Matthew blinked hard against the rain, then pressed the edged of his open left hand against his forehead to shield his eyes. "Where?"

"There. They are walking with intent. They are searching. Damn. They must be armed."

"It's hard to see," said Matthew.

The sky flickered and the ground rumbled with the threat of a forthcoming thunderbolt.

"Pay attention to that change in the dark—that's movement. There it is again," said Simon. "In the distance over there. Do you see it?"

"I do," Thomas whispered, as he came alongside Matthew. "You're right, Simon. I see them. They appear to be searching for prey."

"Then they are searching for us." James rose to his knees and peered over Thomas's left shoulder.

A crack of lightning lit the sky and, for a brief moment, revealed the bandit-scavengers.

"There they are." James was frightened.

Matthew shuddered. "My God."

"Stay down," Simon cautioned. "Yes. We will be their prey if they discover us."

"But we have nothing," Joiada whispered, as he crawled alongside James.

"They seem to be the kind that will rob and kill for nothing," Simon warned.

"How do you know that?" Matthew asked.

"From that last bit of lightning, I caught a glimpse of how close to the ground their heads were bent," Simon explained. "They're scavenging like hungry dogs with nothing to lose."

"Wolves," said Thomas. "Like a pack of wolves."

"More like a pack of hyenas," Simon qualified. "These are truly dangerous hunters."

"They're scavengers," Thomas insisted. "Scavengers."

Together, they leaned toward the outer darkness to monitor this approaching danger.

Plain thunder rolled across the countryside.

"Everybody down," Simon commanded. "Hold still."

"What are we going to do?" Thomas muttered.

"Be still, that's what," Simon demanded. "Damn. I wish I had my dagger."

"Jesus would not have approved of that," said James.

Thomas slapped him on the back. "Jesus is not here."

"Shut up," Simon whispered. "All of you."

Everybody held their breaths and listened.

One of the bandits cackled.

Another spoke. "What is it?"

"I smell meat!"

"Where?"

"I don't know, yet."

"Another streak of lightning might help."

"Hold it!" The dangerous bandits came to a halt. "I smell fear. Spread out."

The bandits could be heard dispersing to the right and to the left. Then they intensified their search after it seemed as if they had established an ill-formed arc.

Simon managed to observe that the bandit at the far right end of the threatening arc was approaching their thicket. "One of them is getting close," he whispered. "Be still."

James almost panicked. "We're going to be found out."

"I said be still, damn you. These scavengers don't know where we here."

The firmament flickered.

Simon picked up a jagged rock. Thomas discovered a stout limb. Matthew found a pointed stick. James grabbed a handful of dirt. Joiada untied his heavy leather belt to use it as a whip.

They waited. They listened. They were prepared to fight.

One of the bandits called out to the others. "Look out! Over there. Look! I see torches."

From a distance, several torches pierced the night.

"Those torches are traveling high and fast," a bandit declared.

"Legionnaires on horseback," another scavenger warned.

The fearless Roman cavalry pushed through the darkness toward the bandits.

"They are onto us!" one of the bandits shouted. "Run!"

They retreated like an infantry unit.

"What are we going to do?" James demanded.

"Be still. Be quiet. Let me listen." Simon assessed the situation. "Good. Those scavengers are moving away from us."

"They are?"

"Yes. Get down. Flat down on the ground. All of you. Down, I say."

Several reports of thunder rumbled across the terrain and accompanied the continuous heavy rain.

"Are you sure . . . sure that all . . . all of them have moved away?" Joiada stammered. "Maybe, maybe there are others nearby that you have not heard."

"Or maybe, the Romans will find us," James offered.

Simon was close to losing his patience. "Be still, you two. That approaching cavalry with their torches *will* find us if you two don't calm down."

"Those Legionnaires are so loud," said James.

"That's on purpose," Simon explained. "They know how to frighten people with fire and noise and galloping speed—especially at night."

Thomas spat into the thicket. "Rotten Rome."

"Be absolutely still," Simon cautioned for the last time. "Those Legionnaires are almost upon us."

From his supine position, James sought after a full astral sky. But to his disappointment, he was given a single pinpoint of light instead. He studied that tiny light, that small heavenly body, which managed to shine through the firmament's gloom above—this steadied his nerves. The others remained calm in whatever way they knew how in order to keep steady in the face of this oncoming danger.

The sound of galloping horses mixed with the blood-thirsty war whoops of the Legionnaire cavalry heralded their fast approach, then denoted their departure after riding by them—dangerously too close.

Simon followed the trajectory of the fast moving Legionnaires and, after a long while, concluded that they were out of danger. "They are riding into the distance."

"Are you sure?"

"Yes, Thomas. Yes."

The general sense of relief was palpable.

The depth of the black night, along with their stillness, had managed to protect them from the bandits, as well as protect them from the dangerous fire of Rome's torches—these threatening lights were often helpless against the vast darkness that often blanketed the Judean countryside.

As time continued to pass within the relative safety of this gloom, they were convinced that they were going to see the light of dawn.

Each disciple discarded his chosen weapon; Joiada secured his heavy leather belt around his waist.

And as more time passed, the discomfort of being wet and cold and hungry and afraid did not penetrate them as deeply.

Eventually, they heard the Legionnaires engage with the bandit-scavengers because, for whatever reason, these scavengers had chosen to flee in a panic and, therefore, call attention to themselves.

Thomas leaned against Simon, then James sat up as Joiada crawled next to Matthew. Together, they listen to the unfolding horror.

The bandit-scavengers pleas for mercy were met with the battle cries of the Legionnaires wielding their hacking swords from their horses. The scavengers' vain pleas were silenced by the efficient and cruel punishment of Rome.

They adjusted their tunics and pulled their mantles over their heads, then leaned downward in response to the harsh wind and the persistent rain. Matthew pressed the edge of his left hand against his forehead to shield his eyes.

Despite the danger that had skirted pass them and despite their continued discomfort, nobody complained, because something in their so-called new found faith gave them the strength to endure this misery.

Thunder and lightning. Wind and Rain.

The night went long for these children of God.

PART X

TOWARD A NEW
BEGINNING

Chapter 38

Daybreak did not feel kind. There was a strange list to the morning clouds—they were not scrubbed clean.

James stood up from within the thicket. It had provided the necessary concealment that he and the others needed throughout their long and dreadful night together.

In response to a mild attack of vertigo, James spread his legs to stabilize his stance. He brushed off dirt from the right side of his face, cleared his throat, and spat dryly into a shrub—he was thirsty.

Matthew coughed after he sat up. "We've escaped Rome, I think."

"For now." James studied the terrain.

Simon sat up and scratched his head. He snorted, then spat on the ground. "Bugs." He stood up and swiped away the gnats that harassed his face.

Thomas stood up, licked his dry lips, then stretched.

Simon released a broken smile. "Are you alright?"

Thomas communicated his misery with a grunt.

Joiada sat up, cracked his neck with a single head-twist to the right, then scrutinized the surrounding men standing and stretching before the presence of dawn. Their arms were extended outward like the barren branches of winter trees.

"I'm hungry," said James.

"There will be food where we are going." Joiada patted his chest. "My purse right here inside my tunic is modest, but I will be able to offer the sheepherder payment if necessary."

"God bless you," said Matthew.

"Please. Think nothing of it." He addressed James. "We do not have to go too far." He grinned. "I'm also hungry."

After they took care of their bodily functions and shook themselves free from their aches and pains and their lack of sleep, a soft blue light descended from the unkind sky and caught their attention.

The light expanded, then intensified before them.

They were transfixed by the depth and the quality of this hue. Then they were startled by an angelic woman, who stepped out from within this enchanting blue light.

She wore a full-length tunic made of pure white undecorated linen. The silk belt, tide around her waist, called attention to her slight figure. A thin line of black hair above her forehead peeked out from underneath the front of her loosely draped upper mantle on her head, which was also draped over her back to cover what must have been a full-length of hair.

Her beautiful face was not veiled.

The quality of her voice was rich and clear and alluring when she finally spoke.

"Our Lord Jesus' body and blood were perfect," she said. "That is why he was offered in sacrifice for your sins, and for the sins of the world. His was not the imperfect body and blood of goats and calves that have had to be sacrificed repeatedly. Jesus' sacrifice does not need to be repeated. It has been done for all time. It is final. It is eternal. The great shepherd was the perfect final sacrifice, made more perfect, through his suffering of God's wrath while he was dying on the cross. All is forgiven by God with your belief in our Lord, Jesus."

The men were captivated by the splendor of her angelic presence, as well as by the absolute significance of her sacred message, which finally, and absolutely, penetrated their hearts and souls.

"Why are you sharing this divine news with us?" James managed to ask.

"We are unworthy," Matthew added, no longer completely paralyzed by this remarkable event. "We are strangers and refugees in this world. We are simply unworthy."

"This is true," she said. "You *are* the sins of the world. But the Messiah has come. He has lived, died, and risen among you forever. Through his sacrifice, you are forgiven once and for all, *all* your sins. God has put you right *through* your faith in your Lord, Jesus Christ. *He* is the means by which your sins are forgiven—*through* your faith in him. This is the final fulfillment of prophecy. This is your salvation. It is God's promise. It is God's will. It has come to pass."

The blue light behind her intensified in such a manner that it forced all five men to shut their eyes.

Matthew pressed the palm of his right hand against his closed eyelids. "We believe, but we don't fully understand this mystery."

"Don't understand," she said. "Surrender yourselves to this mystery—to the Lord, Jesus. Believe in him. Trust in him. Have faith in him. This new covenant is the eternal covenant. And now, you are in union with Christ; you are now his obedient apostles."

After a silent passage of time, the blue light's intensity decreased, which allowed them to open their eyes. They blinked in response to the hue's final dispersion.

The angelic woman had vanished.

James cried, "Where did she go?"

Bedazzled by this ineffable experience, they stood close together in an effort to comprehend the incomprehensible, which had successfully penetrated their hearts and their souls and their minds.

"Was she an angel?" Thomas wondered.

"Or was she someone who was guided by the Holy Spirit?" James speculated.

Simon's continued astonishment prevented him from offering them his opinion.

"She was an angel guided by the Holy Spirit," Matthew submitted, with careful certainty.

"Then what are we waiting for?" James asserted. He placed his right arm upon Joiada's shoulders, who had remained silent and astonished by what he had witnessed, and by what he was presently hearing. "Let us go then. Let us go and join the others."

Matthew placed the palm of his right hand on his chest—over his heart. "So be it."

And so they went, and they walked, toward their careful certainty of today and of tomorrow with their souls filled with faith and anticipation and—they walked, toward a new hope.

They walked, toward the presence of the Risen Christ.

PART XI

BELIEF, AS IT IS—

Chapter 39

Jesus—our Lord and Savior, who died for our sins and gave us everlasting life.

Then God justified us through his saving grace, with our faith in You—Jesus Christ, our redeemer, our salvation; You—who suffered the wrath of God while dying on the cross for our sins, and for the sins of the world—

Jesus, we trust in You.

We love You with all our hearts, souls, and minds.

You—our Lord God, are three persons.

All three persons are fully God.

There is one God.

Each person is equal in being and subordinate in role.

We love You with all our hearts, souls, and minds.

In the name of the Father, the Creator, the Son, the Redeemer, and the Holy Spirit, the Sanctifier—

So be it.

About the Author

D.S. Lliteras is the author of sixteen books that have received national and international acclaim. His short stories and poetry have appeared in numerous magazines, journals, and anthologies. He lives with his wife and author, Kathleen Touchstone.

Praise for the Biblical Novels of D.S. Lliteras

The Master of Secrets

"*Best Genre Fiction of 2007. A mesmerizing story of faith and purpose. Highly recommended for all collections.*"
—Library Journal

"*Lliteras again delivers an imaginatively gripping story.*"
—Publishers Weekly

"*Lliteras continues his chronicles of the Crucifixion . . . Charming tale.*"
—Booklist

"*This is a great work by one of the best early Christian authors.*"
—Midwest Book Review

"*Scenes of stark violence and pure action stand beside dense theological and philosophical dialogues, and occasionally the text reads like a parable.*"
—CBA Retailer+Resources

Jerusalem's Rain

"Top 10 Christian Novel of 2003. Lliteras' great achievement."
—Booklist

"Best Genre Fiction of 2003. Outstanding biblical novel."
—Library Journal

"In Jerusalem's Rain, *D. S. Lliteras completes the author's portrayal of Jesus with a new look at Peter and his anguish."*
—Publishers Weekly

Judas the Gentile

Best Biblical Novel on Amazon—Jungle Find 2016

"Top 10 Christian Novel of 2000. Subtle, provocative."
—Booklist

"Judas' struggle to understand his motives, his faith and his destiny propel the tale."
—Publishers Weekly

"A true work of enduring literature . . ."
—Wisconsin Bookwatch

*"*Judas the Gentile *is so honest and elemental that it seems like the truth."*
—Christian Fiction, A Guide to the Genre (starred review)

The Thieves of Golgotha

Best Biblical Novel on Amazon—Jungle Find 2016

"*Startling, surprisingly successful . . .*"
—*Booklist*

"*Thought-provoking . . . Recommended.*"
—*Library Journal*

"*A sympathetic fictional portrait.*"
—*Publishers Weekly*

"*A tough, vivid, extraordinary novel.*"
—*Christian Fiction, A Guide to the Genre* (starred review)

Descent
The Forty Days After the Crucifixion of Jesus

"*Fans of [Lliteras's] earlier novels will enjoy the fast pace of [Descent] and his insistence of portraying ordinary people.*"
—*Booklist*

"*This is yet another work by D.S. Lliteras that provokes a stringent 'YES!' from the reader. He sees the world as few are able, and shares the meaning of feeling with us. Quite simply, this is a brilliant little novel—especially for those who struggle with the concepts of sainthood and how it happens.*"
—*The San Francisco Review of Books*